RUN & HIDE

A DARK HALLOWEEN ROMANCE

ANNIE WILD

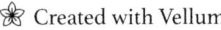

CONTENT WARNING

This is a dark stepsibling romance and while not as heavy as some of my other works, it still contains some themes that some readers may find disturbing. You will find the following: stalking, graphic sex, violence, attempted sexual assault (not between main characters), taboo relationships, verbal abuse/bullying, and childhood trauma.

To the readers who'd love to live in a picturesque, forever-autumn town and the thought of a sexy, dominate asshole haunting them is exciting.
Happy Halloween, Shy Girls.

1

SHILOH

WHOEVER DECIDED to start telling teenagers *'it gets better after high school'* was lying through their teeth...

At least when it comes to me.

Unfortunately, I still have to sit across from the same chick who declared to the whole senior class my prom dress looked like it was puked up by a seasick alien...and you know what?

Nothing has changed. Melanie is still shooting me daggers and rolling her eyes with every suggestion I make. I'm still white knuckling this ballpoint pen and imagining what it would be like to gouge her eyes out with it. So, while I guess we pay taxes and have mortgages now, the hierarchy of the mean girl transcends beyond the diploma I received from Avalon High School.

Well, and my Bachelor's in Education.

And Master's in English.

Why did I decide to become a teacher in my home town again?

"Um, earth to Shiloh?" Melanie snaps her perfectly manicured nails in my face. "Did you hear that I was asking for suggestions? You're literally a bottomless pit of catchy phrases, and no one else can come up with anything."

"What about 'Legends and Lore'?" I pipe up, pretending like I've been paying attention this entire time. "We could have a costume contest based on local ghost stories, set up interactive reenactments of the town's history, maybe even hold an auction for 'cursed' antiques? It would be a true cele-bration of Avalon's historic character that inspired our Halloween Ball in the first place. This town is a picturesque representation of almost everyone's fall Pinterest boards."

For a prolonged moment, there's only silence, while I try to tamp down the rare enthusiasm that bubbles out of me whenever I discuss this topic. I see a few of my fellow committee members nodding, considering my suggestion and sparking a little hope in me that we might pull off some-thing really cool this year. That is, until Melanie's patronizing laugh shatters my dream like biting through the hard shell of a candy apple.

"Oh, Shiloh," she titters, shaking her head at me like I'm a child who just said something adorably naïve. "We can't expect our most affluent donors to get excited about dusty old fairy tales. No, we need something more trendy, more sophisticated. You know what I just thought of? *Masquerade of the Macabre.* Everyone loves a mask theme. It's sexy, mysteri-ous. Of course, we'll have a costume contest, but I don't want to be judging droves of pilgrim hats and stained nightgowns. How dull would that be?"

"There will be *children* there," I remind her, biting my tongue so hard I taste copper. I want to argue about setting a good example for my high school students–but she'd be mute to that point, I'm sure.

"Um, there will still be a dress code," she laughs in that same condescending tone.

I keep my mouth shut, knowing the battle is lost. It doesn't matter that most of our "affluent donors" consist of elders, whose families have lived here for generations and would probably have loved the idea to celebrate our spooky, lore-ridden history. Not to mention, all that *lore* is the foundation of our whole damn tourism trade. But I know that would be pointless. Melanie's mind is made up, and not even a thousand spiced lattes would give me the energy required to enter that wrestling match.

"So, what are we going to do about the funding crisis?" A voice speaks up. I miss who throws it out there, but I *don't* miss the 'funding crisis' part. What are they talking about?

"Well, I'm afraid I have some truly terrible news on that front..." Melanie dramatically sighs. "Bellman's Orchards have pulled out as our principal sponsor. Apparently, their summer profits were not what they'd hoped for. We're facing a significant budget shortfall for the epic bash I intend to pull together, so we really need to find an alternative fast."

The room erupts into a cacophony of gasps and anxious murmuring. You'd think she'd just announced the End of Days rather than a hiccup in party planning.

"Now, now, everyone," Melanie says, raising her hands in a preachy gesture that makes me want to throw my notebook at her head. "Let's not jump straight to panicking. As my father always says, '*there's no problem that can't be solved with a simple plan B and a bit of elbow grease.*' All we need to do is brainstorm other businesses who could come up with a lump of cash and do so quickly."

Oh really, Mel? A simple plan B in the form of a pile of money?

There can be no doubt in anyone's mind that our committee chairman has absorbed every ounce of wisdom her father has fed her with his favorite silver spoon. Her father is the mayor of this town, and some say the wealthiest. Others say they're up to their heads in debt. Maybe that's why she's not offering to front it herself? I can't imagine her passing up the chance to save the day.

Regardless, the next fifteen minutes are a mind-numbing blur of increasingly hopeless suggestions. Local businesses are named and dismissed faster than a speed-dating event for escaped convicts. I doodle spiderwebs absentmindedly in the margins of my notes, wondering if there's a circle of Hell dedicated entirely to committee meetings.

"We have to think bigger, people. Hey, Shiloh, what about your brother?" Melanie's voice cuts through my daydreaming of fiery pits like a bucket of ice water. I look up, momentarily confused. My brother–well, *half*-brother–is six years old. Melanie must be mistaking me for somebody else. But she doesn't seem to think so, because she's still staring at me with that predatory gleam in her eye I remember all too well from our years at school.

"Isn't his father some big shot in New York?" she presses, lacing her pink-taloned fingers together and leaning forward. I instantly wish she'd go back to pretending I don't exist. "Blackwood Enterprises, right? They must be loaded."

The pen in my hand creaks as my grip tightens enough to almost snap it in two. "Oh...um. You mean Dominic? My step-brother? We, uh...we're not exactly close."

Understatement of the century right there. Dominic and I are about as close as the North and South Poles, our relationship just as warm. But Melanie is like a dog with a particularly juicy bone, if said dog was maybe a mutant and resembled something more akin to a T-rex. She's not letting this one go.

"Oh, come on, Shiloh. This is for the good of the community, for our school. You wouldn't want to let your students down, would you?"

And there it is, folks. The signature Melanie manipulation, dressed up in community spirit and accessorized with just enough guilt to make you feel like a selfish asshole if you even *think* about saying no. I glance around the room, met with the hopeful stares of each of my fellow committee members in turn. The last time I was looked at like this, like the human embodiment of salvation, I had just offered my freshman class an open-book exam for their final last year.

"Okay, I'll try," I grit out, the oath tasting like ash in my mouth. "But don't expect any miracles. Dominic isn't exactly known for his generosity."

Or his community spirit, or penchant for philanthropy, or possession of a beating fucking heart.

Melanie claps her hands together with an ear-splitting squeal, her expression dripping with shameless triumph. "Wonderful! I knew we could count on you for *something*, Shiloh."

I press my lips together in a pathetic excuse for a smile and slouch down in my chair, already regretting my promise. By the time the meeting finally adjourns, I'm convinced I've developed a stomach ulcer the size of a prize pumpkin.

I grumble to myself all the way home, beyond irritated

that I let Melanie get to me. This is just like that time she convinced our group in eighth-grade chemistry that *I* should do our entire midterm project by myself, because I was the smartest and anyone else's contribution could just bring our grade down.

Nothing. Ever. Changes.

By the time I make it through my front door, I'm a storm of bitter rage. I slam it closed behind me and throw my purse to the ground as if doing so could release even the tiniest fraction of my frustration.

No such luck.

I'm anxious and seething and I'd punch a hole through my wall if I thought I had the money or skill to fix it again afterwards. But I don't, so I resort to pacing back and forth through my tiny living room, chewing on my thumb nail while my cell phone feels like a lead weight in my other hand.

"Get a grip, Shiloh," I mutter to myself. "It's just a phone call. To the Manhattan office of your estranged stepbrother. No big deal. He'll say *no* and hang up, and we can all forget this stupid idea was ever born."

I take a deep breath and hit the call button before I can chicken out. Of course, I had to Google the number for the reception desk. Dominic Blackwood isn't saved to anyone's contacts in this town. The ringing seems to go on forever, or maybe it only trills a few times? My heart is pounding too loud to decipher the difference.

"Blackwood Enterprises, how may I help?"

Fuck. It's really happening.

"Um, hi," I try desperately to swallow around the thick wedge of anxiety stuck in my throat. "I'm trying to reach

Dominic Blackwood. Could you redirect me to his office, please?"

"I'm sorry, Mr. Blackwood doesn't accept external calls that haven't gone through his assistant. Would you like her extension? I'm sure she can schedule a call for you when Mr. Blackwood has space in his itinerary."

"No, no, thank you. Please just put me through to Dominic. I'm his...I'm his sister. Tell him it's Shiloh, he'll take the call."

There's a pause on the other end, I can practically hear the receptionist raising her eyebrow, contemplating whether or not to just hang up on me.

Please, do. Then I can tell everyone I tried.

"One moment, please. I'll ring up to his office now."

Double fuck.

Hold music suddenly blares from my phone speaker. It's some generic jazz that sounds like it was composed by an AI with a vendetta against human ears–and I resume my pacing. Rapidly running out of thumbnail to chew on, my free hand finds its way into my hair, nervously tugging at the tendrils that have fallen loose from my haphazard bun.

"Well, well, Shy Girl. To what do I owe the displeasure?"

I freeze mid-step as that voice, cool and controlled, rakes down my spine as if he were standing in this very room. My jaw automatically clenches at the stupid nickname he used to taunt me with when we were preteens. I don't respond immediately, my mouth suddenly drier than an ancient tome in Avalon's haunted Fairchild Manor library.

"Hello?" he prompts, impatient as ever. "I don't have all day. I can *hear* you breathing."

I close my eyes and swallow the embarrassment. "Yeah,

Dominic, hi. I'm here." I cringe almost to the point of pain as I stammer through my greeting. I'm already picturing him leaning back in some fancy leather desk chair, probably wondering what cosmic joke has led to this mortifying encounter.

"Yes, okay, now we've covered that part," he throatily chuckles. "You're the one who made the call. Get to it, I'm busy."

My head just keeps spinning as I try to conjure up a coherent sentence. "Yeah, uh, sorry. I'm calling about...about the Avalon Halloween Ball? I don't know if you remember it. But, um...our sponsor pulled out and now we're having some major funding issues, and I was sorta hoping..."

"Let me get this straight," Dominic cuts in, every word laced with disdain. "We haven't spoken to each other in *years*. And now you're calling me, out of the blue, to ask for money? For a *costume* party?"

Alright, dude. Put it like that and of course *it sounds ridiculous.*

I run my hand through my hair again, fighting the urge to rip every last strand from my scalp. "It's not just some costume party. It's a fundraiser for the school–the one I teach English at. And it's...it's tradition. Keeping town spirit alive and...and *stuff*."

"Town spirit and stuff," he repeats slowly, as if talking to a patient with late-stage dementia. "How quaint. I'm sure my father would be thrilled to throw company money at such a noble and vital cause. Really saving lives, aren't you?"

"Dominic, *please*," I huff, hating beyond measure the desperate note that's crept into my voice unchecked. "I wouldn't have called if we had any other options. This is not easy for me, and you know it. The school is really struggling right now, these are my students I'm trying to help. Also, it wasn't my idea. Melanie–"

"Melanie is a bitch."

Huh, okay. That's the one thing we can agree on.

Before I can say anything though, he continues. "I have *actual* work to do. Work that doesn't involve throwing parties for small-town, hopeless cases like yours. Goodbye, Shy Girl."

I pull the phone from my ear, and double check that he did, indeed, just hang up on me. "Well, that went about as well as expected," I mumble, plopping down on my couch.

I don't know at what point I'd started to actually hope, but here I lie, thoroughly and suddenly disappointed–as if there was even the slightest chance my soulless stepbrother might actually do something kind. But honestly, *anyone* other than me stood a better chance at getting him to bend. He's always been a jerk to me.

A fucking bully, to be precise.

I scrub my hands down my face, watching the swirls in the crumbling plaster of my ceiling morph into blackholes of despair. As much as I hate to admit it...

The Avalon Halloween Ball is my favorite day of the year.

Bitchy Melanie or not. Rich sponsor or not. I have to find a way to save it, resorting to desperate measures if I have to. Maybe it *is* time to try the whole black altar thing...

I'm startled out of my witchy musings by my cell vibrating right next to my face. Narrowly avoiding falling right off the couch, I snatch it up and swipe at the screen. I'm greeted by a text message from an unsaved number.

UNKNOWN: I'LL MEET YOU TOMORROW. 1PM.
THE COFFEE HOUSE BY THE OLD CHURCH.
DON'T BE LATE.

I blink several times, reading the message over and over as if it will eventually make better sense. Did I accidentally summon some kind of bossy demon just by *thinking* about attempting black magic?

Am I a witch?

"The fuck...? Dominic?"

It can't be. That wouldn't make any sense. Why would he change his mind literally two minutes after dismissing me? And why would he bother to drive more than a couple hours to Avalon just to meet me for coffee?

Well, then again...

He's *always* gone the extra mile to torture me.

2

DOMINIC

THE WINDING ROADS of Avalon are a far cry from the towering skyscrapers and crammed sidewalks of Manhattan. As I drive at a snail's pace through the narrow lanes, past the storefronts that look like they haven't changed since the 1800s, I'm reminded why I was so relieved to put this whole town in my rearview in the first place. The air of numb complacency is suffocating, clinging to every person, building, and fucking tree like a thick fog.

Everybody's grandma knows everybody's grandma, and they're all perfectly content with just being small-minded, small-town people. Fuck, just the *idea* of growing old in a place like this is enough to make me physically ill...

So why did I even come to this town full of irreverent people?

Oh, yeah. *Her.*

I arrive at the coffee house twenty minutes early, parking across the street where I have a clear view of the entrance. The building is an old, converted church, its weathered stone façade now adorned with a bright, tacky sign reading '*Heavenly Brews*'.

I roll my eyes at the painfully unoriginal pun, just like I used to do every time I passed it as a teenager. The bad joke is almost as ridiculous as the fact that this place is an old church, but everyone in town knows it as the coffee house *by* the old church. That's because it sits beside the crumbling ruins of an even older church, complete with glassless windows and an overgrown graveyard.

So many churches in such a small place.

I check my watch for the fifth time in as many minutes, drumming my fingers impatiently on my steering wheel as I warily eye the cobbled street that stretches before me. The urge to start the car and head straight back to my city is a lingering temptation, though not as strong as the one to stay.

Just as I'm about to write both impulses off completely, a flash of golden hair catches my eye. My heart stutters in my chest as I watch a young woman who can only be Shiloh march down the street, a reluctant sort of determination in her every step.

She's something entirely different from the awkward teenager I remember, yet undeniably familiar. Her hair is pulled back in a messy ponytail, a chaos of escaping strands framing her face as if meant to tell the world she doesn't give a damn about her appearance. Yet, the effect is frustratingly appealing.

I, myself, have a certain appetite for reducing a woman to an artful kind of mess.

My gaze travels down her body, spurred on by primal curiosity. The years have been kind to my little Shy Girl, filling out soft curves in all the right places. Even in simple jeans and a worn leather jacket that I'm pretty sure was handed down from her dad, she looks good enough to eat.

Fuck, it's been years since I've seen her.

She was fifteen back then, just a year younger than I was when my own father requested that I go and live with him in New York. I was always taller than her when we were kids, but now, eleven years later, I stand at a healthy six-three. When we're face to face once again, I know that I'll tower over her five-foot-four-ish frame.

A sudden, unbidden thought flashes through my mind as I watch her approach the coffee house. A forbidden musing on how easy it would be to pick her up, throw her around a bit maybe. She looks like a fragile little thing I'd very much enjoy toying with. I wonder what it'd be like to devour her...

We wrestled sometimes as kids. Or rather, I'd chase her and pin her down. She always claimed she hated our silly game, but I knew differently. I could see the thrill in her eyes every time. Perhaps if I hadn't moved away, if we'd carried on playing for a couple more years, I might have done more to feed my addiction, seeing that look on her flushed face. I've never seen its allure matched in any woman I've pinned down since.

I shake my head and force a frustrated exhale through my nose. I left that messy confusion behind me a long time ago.

Shiloh hesitates at the door to the coffee house, her shoulders rising and falling as if she's taking her own deep breath. I allow myself a small smirk.

Good. I hope she's nervous. It was always fun to watch my Shy Girl stumble.

Unable to resist any longer, I slip out of my car and cross the street, timing my arrival so I reach the door just as she's pulling it open. She nearly jumps out of her skin as my fingers close around the bar above hers. I try and fail to not relish her stunned little yelp.

"You're late," I say by way of greeting, keeping my tone clipped and distant. She doesn't need to know I was craving this moment the entire two and a half hours it took me to drive here.

Her sharp, ice-blue eyes narrow. "I was late by like, two minutes," she snaps. "And for the record, it's nice to see you too, Dom."

I don't respond, simply holding the door open with an expression of exaggerated expectation, as if I'm not sure she knows that these things were originally invented for walking through. She rolls her eyes and stalks inside with a loud scoff, making her way to a vacant table in the corner of the almost-empty establishment.

And just like that, I'm reliving my old favorite hobby. *Pissing her the fuck off.*

An awkward silence settles over us both as we sit. I lean back in my chair, adopting an air of bored indifference while I covertly study her. Shiloh fidgets with the zipper on her jacket for a full minute before finally shrugging it off and signaling the waitress for two cups of shitty coffee. Her uncomfortable squirming and avoidance of eye contact give me ample opportunity to rake my gaze over her T-shirt clad chest.

"So, um...how's New York?" she finally stutters, the feeble attempt at small talk grating on my nerves already.

"Let's skip the pleasantries." I dismiss the question with a swipe of my hand through the air. I haven't bothered to take off my own thick overcoat, or my black leather gloves–a fact that seems to snare Shiloh's attention. "I'm not here for a cozy catch up."

Her plump lips press together into a thin line that has me immediately missing their fullness. Eventually she nods, taking another deep breath before starting again. "Right. Well, about the Halloween Ball–"

"I didn't come to talk about that either," I interrupt, taking a perverse kind of pleasure in watching her hopeful expression dissipate, and then shift to barely concealed rage.

"Then why did you come, huh?" she blurts out. "Why drive all this way just to tell me to forget about it? *Again?*" The way she spits at me through her teeth is fucking delicious.

I shrug, letting my own lips curve slightly into a mocking smirk. "The way you begged me over the phone made it sound like the town was crumbling down around your ears. I figured I would pass through and see for myself. Perhaps Blackwood Enterprises is interested in bulldozing the whole thing and building a bunch of warehouses. You know...something more *useful*."

"I did not beg," she says incredulously, missing the rest of my insult to her pitiful little forever-autumn town.

"Oh, Shy Girl, I *beg* to differ." I chuckle, unable to stop myself as that familiar enraged flush creeps up her cheeks.

Oh yeah, this was worth the drive.

She glares at me. "This isn't a joke, Dom. The school really needs–"

"The school's financial circumstances are not my concern," I cut her off again, certain if I do it one more time, her head might actually explode. "Nor are your pathetic, small town traditions."

"They are not pathetic," Shiloh argues, leaning forward

with a sudden furious intensity that almost catches me off guard. "The Halloween Ball has been a part of Avalon's community calendar for more than a hundred years. It's a celebration of our collective history and something that brings everyone together. And my students *need* it as much as everyone else loves it." She takes in a long, hefty breath, and then opens her mouth to say more.

I hold up a hand. "Really? Do you have *more* to add to this heartfelt spiel?"

More daggers come from her pretty blue eyes. "Seriously, Dom, even *you* have to admit that everyone's lot in life is propped up on the quality of their education. That was your whole fucking shtick, wasn't it? Before you *escaped*." She punctuates the end of her tirade with air quotes, throwing in my face the memory of how I used to rant to our parents about our shitty high school and its shitty facilities.

Hmm. It seems as though nothing ever really changes.

Shiloh's eyes still glow with that blue flame any time she gets into a passion vent about something. She used to always find any excuse to yell at me from some fucking soapbox or other. Before I left, I found myself starting to enjoy her rambling. But of course, that was before I came to my senses– and shoved those thoughts where they belong, beneath even my darkest layers. They're trembling inside of me now, reminding me of what I left behind.

Maybe this was a bad idea.

But I swallow it. "Yes, yes, that's all very touching," I say, lacing my words with as much condescension as possible. "Poor, lonely Shy Girl, on her own for so long she's desperate just to be a part of something. You're like a nauseating Hallmark movie trying to save this fucking party of yours. Doesn't change the fact that it's not *my* problem. Blackwood Enterprises is not a charity. We don't throw money at bullshit lost causes."

The flash of hurt in her eyes is unmistakable, even as she tries to mask it with outrage. "Lost causes, huh? That's what you still think of all of us here? Of me?" Her voice wavers a little this time, some of that bite softening as she questions my disregard for everything she clearly holds so dear.

Seeing her start to crumble so quickly is immediately boring.

Pathetic. It's a shame really. Shiloh was always a smart girl, she could have done almost anything she wanted if she'd grown a fucking backbone and left this town for longer than it took her to get some worthless degrees at the nearest irrelevant college.

I refuse to pity her for making stupid life choices.

"What I think," I answer, standing abruptly, "is that this was a waste of time. You need to grow the fuck up, Shiloh. This town is a worthless smudge on the map of a much wider world that's leaving *you* behind."

I stalk out without bothering to wait for a response. It would likely be weak and stuttered anyway. Little Shy Girl, still *so* disappointing.

And yet, as I climb into my car, I can't quite name whatever impulse is holding me hostage as I fail to put the Mercedes in drive, once again watching the damn door of the coffeehouse. I tell myself I just want to enjoy that defeated look on her face a little longer. That I'll be immensely satisfied to witness how her purposeful steps will have morphed into a sad dawdle when she finally drags herself from that table.

I'm momentarily distracted from my vigil by an incessant buzzing from inside my coat pocket. Fishing out my cell, I grind my teeth a little at the string of messages I find from my father.

DAD: WHAT'S THIS I HEAR ABOUT YOU LEAVING
THE CITY?

DAD: I DIDN'T GIVE YOU PERMISSION TO TAKE
TIME OFF.

DAD: TURN YOUR SORRY ASS AROUND AND
GET BACK HERE.

DAD: I HAVE TASKS THAT REQUIRE YOUR
IMMEDIATE ATTENTION.

I close my eyes and force another deep inhale, in serious danger of cracking a molar if I don't get myself under control. I deserve some time off.

For all my lofty privileges and army of subordinates at the firm, I'm barely more than a glorified enforcer for my CEO father. My extensive capabilities are sorely wasted while I spend my days following his every order. Dante Blackwood couldn't give less of a fuck about my ideas for the future of our company.

No, until my name is written in the top spot, all he wants me to think about is whatever he *commands* me to think about. More often than not, he has me thinking about how to make sure everyone else is also following his orders. Quickly and fearfully and without fucking question.

Maybe it's some petty kind of late-stage rebellion that has me now emailing my assistant to cancel the rest of my week. Maybe it's the intoxicating allure of watching my pretty little sister squirm some more.

Whatever the cause, all I know is that I feel the need to

stick around in dear, old Avalon a little longer. And when Shiloh finally makes her exit from the coffee house, leather-clad arms wrapped around herself as she wanders back in the direction she came from, some phantom instinct has me turning my key in the ignition.

Just this once, I tell myself. *I'll probably be bored of her tomorrow.*

But right now, all I desire to do is follow her.

3

SHILOH

I TRUDGE BACK HOME with a stomach full of leaden disappointment. The crisp fall air does absolutely nothing to cool my burning rage as I kick at fallen leaves with every step.

Who the fuck does he think he is? That condescending asshole!

My focus is so intent on scorching the sidewalk with my glare, I almost bump into a lamppost when my phone suddenly starts buzzing in my pocket. I pull it out, more than ready to hit ignore on whoever dares interrupt my tantrum. But the moment I see the caller ID, I swipe to answer with a defeated sigh.

"Hey, Grey. Happy Saturday."

"Well, damn," my friend and fellow teacher, Greyson, chuckles through the speaker. "Who shit in your cornflakes this morning? Unlike you to be in such a rotten mood."

"A ghost of dismal Halloween's past," I grumble, still clueless as to what magical revelation I'm supposed to have in order to save that of the present. "Would you believe me if I said yesterday's meeting with Avalon's most entitled bitch wasn't actually the worst encounter of my weekend so far?"

"*Jeez*, I didn't think there was anyone in town capable of outdoing Melanie on that front. What happened?"

"I don't even know where to start, but at this rate, my head might explode before Monday rolls around."

Greyson laughs again, the deep boom of it bouncing around my skull and helping to drown out the echoes of Dominic's cutting remarks. "As it happens, you little drama gremlin, I was calling to ask if you wanna head to The Cauldron tonight? You sound like you're in need of a stiff drink."

I hesitate, my plans before answering the call having been to stomp home and wallow by myself. However, a night of drinking and dancing with my friends at my favorite spooky-themed tavern might be just what I need to convince myself that life here in Avalon isn't as depressing as my snobby stepbrother seems to think it is.

"Yeah," I finally answer. "Sounds like a plan. Who else is coming? Did you text the group chat?"

"Oh, um, no not yet. You're the only person I've asked. I'll, uh, drop a line in there now." Greyson's slightly reluctant response has me raising an eyebrow, though I know he can't see it. I choose not to question him, my thoughts wandering instead through a number of outfit choices I'll need to narrow down once I make it home.

"Cool, I'll see you there then. Laters, Grey." I hang up before anything grows awkward.

Several hours and one meager PB&J later, I'm pushing through the heavy oak door of The Cauldron, a mechanical witch's cackle greeting my arrival. I'm immediately enveloped by the familiar warmth of the old place, soothing the gooseflesh that pebbles beneath my fishnets from the late September chill outside. An easy grin spreads across my cheeks as I seek out my friends in the crowd of costumed patrons and masked staff carrying trays of smoking cocktails.

Coming here will always make any crappy day feel better.

I spot Greyson's towering figure at a table in the corner with several members of our Avalon High group chat, a motley crew of would-be loners who have very little in common beyond our workplace but love each other all the same. This is something Dominic will never understand–the quiet comfort of being surrounded by people who appreciate our cozy, 'worthless smudge on the map' as much as I do.

"Shiloh, you made it!" Greyson pulls me in for a one-armed hug. "Jemma was just filling us in on your sponsor issue, no wonder you sounded so grumpy on the phone!"

"Ugh, don't remind me, please," I answer with a grimace. "My plan tonight is to get drunk enough that I stop thinking about the disaster of it all."

"I figure the call with your brother didn't go so well then?" Jemma asks, worriedly eyeing me over the top of a goblet of red wine.

"My *stepbrother*, thank you very much. I don't share blood with that demon. And no, you could say it went about as well as if I had asked him to dress up as a cockerel and nail himself to my roof."

Greyson cringes and sucks air through his teeth with a pained hiss. "Sounds like a jolly family reunion. Let me get you a pint," he offers, patting me on the back before weaving his way to the bar. I smooth out my black skirt and matching crop top as he walks away, pleasantly surprised with how well my look came together.

"Well, I guess it's back to the drawing board then," Jemma mumbles, staring into her drink. "Should have known we shouldn't get our hopes up for a knight in tailored Tom Ford."

I laugh loudly despite the general gloom of it all, winding my arm around Jemma as she huffs her own muted giggle. Our timid librarian has never met Dominic, having moved to town years after he'd left for New York, but she's hit the nail on the head with that apt description. No doubt she's picturing her own corporate tormentor when she envisions a villain in a suit. The oldest of our group at thirty-nine, Jemma moved to Avalon five years ago after a messy divorce from a tax accountant, cheating bastard. As far as any of us know, she's sworn off men for good in favor of books and quiet solitude.

A cause I can get behind, that's for sure.

"Honestly Jem, if I were to describe Dominic as a knight, he'd have to be one of the Knights Templar. You know, rich and self-righteous and crusading through town just to leave a bloody mess in his wake." I squeeze her shoulder as the rest of our group chuckles at my dark joke.

"Wait, I thought he hadn't been in town for more than a decade?" Luke asks, the beefy gym teacher nursing his own pint.

"Oh yeah, get this," I start, shaking my head. "He slammed me with a resounding *fuck off* over the phone last night, and then drove more than two hours this morning just to do it all over again in person. I mean what a *psycho*, am I right?" I feel royally vindicated as I'm met with incredulous stares from each of my friends in turn. Even people who didn't grow up with Dominic as a constant shadow in their home can agree he's a raging jerk.

"I don't get it. What possible reason could he have for being such an asshole to his own family?" Ruby pipes up. My fellow English teacher is the newest addition to our ranks, having only started at the school at the beginning of this semester. The closest to my age, and obviously sharing the fierce passion Jemma and I have for literature, Ruby is someone I hope to become good friends with in time. I can't say I ever had a best friend growing up. These days the closest I have are Greyson and Luke, but they have their own bromance going on that I never feel fully a part of.

"Oh, honey, let me debrief you on the drama as succinctly as possible. *Basically,* Dominic's mom cheated on his rich and successful father with *my* poor and lowly mechanic dad, and then forced him to move here to this middle-of-nowhere town when he was twelve. He's never forgiven her for it and has hated everyone and everything in this place ever since, including me."

"*Yikes*, that's a messy story," Ruby says with a wry smile. "But still, it's not like any of it was your fault. Why would Dominic bear such a grudge against *you* that he'd go to the effort of driving all the way here just to upset you?"

"Eh, he's just a miserable grouch and always has been. He gets off on inflicting suffering," I answer with a dismissive wave of my hand. "I don't know if it's because I came as an unwelcome package deal with my dad when our parents got married, or because he hates all women, or because he's just the spawn of Satan–but I endured a peachy four years of constant torture before he moved back to New York and left us all in peace."

"And good riddance!" Greyson toasts from behind me, placing down a pint of my favorite rich stout. I can't count the number of hours we've spent bonding over childhood trauma since Greyson fled his own screwed-up family to find some quiet relief in Avalon. I guess most of my fellow townsfolk who didn't grow up here settled in our little patch of nowhere precisely because it was such a stark contrast to whatever chaos they needed to escape elsewhere.

"Here, here!" I raise my drink to my lips and take a long pull of the dark ale. "If it's alright with everyone else, I'd like to pretend none of it ever happened for the rest of the evening."

"I'll drink to that," Ruby chimes in, raising her brightly colored cocktail. "Come on, Shy, let's go dance. You're in need of distraction."

The DJ puts on an upbeat remix of *Thriller* and suddenly I'm being pulled through a writhing mass of sweaty bodies and into the middle of the dance floor. I laugh and sway with the rest of them, eagerly accepting several more drinks as my friends band together to take my mind off Dominic's assholery and the looming peril of our beloved Halloween Ball.

By the time it's my turn to get the next round, I'm tripping over my own feet a little as I make my way to the bar. Strong hands steady me and I look up to see Greyson's flushed cheeks spread in an amused grin. "You okay?" he yells over the music.

"Never better!" I answer, an almost maniacal giggle bubbling up from my throat.

I continue pushing through the crowd, Greyson's hand a steady warmth on my back as he supervises my mission to stay upright. The coolness of the polished wooden bar feels wonderful against the blazing heat of my skin, and I have to resist the urge to lay my cheek on it while we wait for a bartender's attention.

"So," Greyson starts, after I've bellowed our drinks order over the pulsing beat. "Any ideas for an alternate sponsor?"

I groan, pinching the bridge of my nose between my fingers and thumb. "Can we not talk about it right now? I told you I wanted to not think for one evening."

"Sorry, sorry," he hurriedly responds, holding up his hands like I've raised a weapon in his direction. "I just hate seeing you miserable. You know I'm always here if you need anything, right?"

I lift my head, offering him a grateful smile. "I know. You're a good friend, Grey. Maybe I'll bounce some ideas off you next week if you have the time." I twist back to the bar, pulling out my card to pay for our drinks, suddenly very aware of Greyson's hand still resting on the small of my back. Before I can open my mouth to question him on it, a masked server appears to our side, depositing a fully laden tray of empty glasses on the bar.

Time seems to slow as the precarious cargo nudges the fresh pint sat in front of Greyson, tipping it sideways until the glass topples over completely. I leap out of the way with a yelp, narrowly avoiding the spray of frothy lager. Greyson isn't so lucky as he reflexively snaps his hand out to catch the glass before it rolls to the floor. The narrow save leaves him right in the splash zone.

"Damn, sorry, dude," the server mumbles from behind his zombie mask. "Let me get you a rag or something."

Greyson can only gape at the dark wet patch that's

seeping into his crotch before snapping his gaze up to see the server disappearing into the crowd. Try as I might, I can't hold back the snorting cackle that bursts from my lips at his baffled expression, not to mention the sorry state of his pants.

"Oh, you think this is funny, do you?" he demands, trying to maintain a stern expression but failing miserably as he huffs his own embarrassed laugh. He shakes his head. "Well, I'm glad my misfortune entertains you."

"Aw, sorry, Grey. Let me get you another drink." I bite my lip to stifle another bout of giggles.

"Nah, don't worry about it. I think I'm gonna call it a night, wet jeans are the worst." He sighs, looking down again at his soaked crotch before turning to presumably seek out the vanished server. "Get home safe, okay?"

"Will do," I chirp, giving him an awkward hug while trying to avoid any of the mess seeping into my own clothes. As I watch him leave, I realize the room is starting to spin, the masked faces of staff and patrons alike blurring into a nightmarish kaleidoscope. If I were being smart right now, I'd leave too. But fuck being smart, I figure I have space for at least another two pints before I stumble home. Well, I'll have that room, right after I empty my straining bladder.

I holler at Luke to come and relieve me of everyone else's drinks and then clumsily maneuver my way through the dancing masses and towards the restroom. The night is still young, and I'm not yet drunk enough to completely wipe Dominic's smirking face from my mind.

4

DOMINIC

An Hour Earlier...

The embarrassingly kitsch bar is heaving when I slip inside just a few minutes after Shiloh, and the sea of masks and drunken losers provide excellent cover while I keep an eye on my scantily clad little sister.

I have no excuse to be here. I know what I'm doing is verging on unhinged. But having spent too many monotonous hours parked in a sheltered space down the street from her house, all I can think is that I was a little out of my mind with boredom by the time she strode out of her door. Wrapped in that daring little black outfit and fishnets, it felt like she was practically begging for me to follow.

As soon as the door of The Cauldron swings shut behind me, I swipe up a discarded mask from a nearby table and pull it on. I've already abandoned my coat, blazer, and shirt in my car, certain I'll blend in easier in just a T-shirt and slacks.

Fuck knows what I'd say if she caught me here, in a shitty rubber mask of all things.

My eyes lock onto Shiloh almost immediately, tucked away in a corner with what I presume is her little gaggle of small town friends. I skirt the room, slowly making my way closer until I can lean against a wooden pillar that stands just behind their table.

My frown steadily deepens until there's a slight ache forming between my brows as she regales her sob story about what a horrible person I am to her rapt audience. The venom dripping from her every word ignites something primal within me.

Why the hell would she paint me as such a soulless villain in her life story, as if I didn't endure my own suffering during our *oh-so-sunny* childhood?

But also, there's a twisted sense of satisfaction brimming with my irritation. It's clear that I've gotten under my little Shy Girl's skin. In fact, it seems I burrowed under there many years ago and haven't left.

The anger steadily fades to amusement as she continues on her tirade, her friends nodding in sycophantic agreement. What a sad little clique, drowning their insecurities in cheap beer and indignation at the world that's too big and scary for them. I almost feel sorry for them.

Almost.

Shiloh can rant and rave all she wants, but she has no idea what *real* torment feels like. Perhaps it's time she learned? After all, I consider myself something of a specialist in the field, and what kind of older brother would I be if I didn't teach my little sis some harsh truths?

I keep to my shadowy corner, the blackened cogs turning in my mind while I watch Shiloh dance with her friends and get more sloppily drunk by the minute. It's not until one of the guys lays his hands on her that I feel compelled to abandon my post as a silent bystander.

Tracking their movements through the tiny holes in my mask, I almost lose sight of Shiloh and her overly familiar friend as they make their way toward the bar. For some inexplicable reason, the casual hand he's placed on the small of her back has me choking back a boiling rage.

I tell myself I just want to fuck with Shiloh as I grab a nearby tray loaded with empty glasses from an abandoned table. At best, I might rid her of that supportive presence that's ready to catch her should she fall on her drunk ass. At worst, maybe I'll cockblock her shot at getting lucky with the one pathetic lowlife in this place showing her any interest.

I stalk toward the bar after them, repeating my reasons in my head. I'm only picturing ripping that hand from her body by whatever means necessary because I want to sap her of whatever enjoyment she might be getting from the touch.

Lo and behold, my plan works perfectly. One clumsy knock of the tray and I send a full pint toppling into the guy's lap. Shame I didn't manage to catch Shiloh in the crossfire, but those perfectly polished Doc Martens will be nice and sticky come morning. I mumble a half-hearted apology and make my escape, careful to disguise my voice in case she should recognize it.

Not that there was much danger of Shiloh making that deduction. She's absolutely wasted, her cheeks flushed an almost luminous pink and her sweaty hair damp and curling at her temples. It's hard not to imagine that she might look a similar state after a long and thorough fucking.

I huff an exasperated sigh, banishing the thought before it's burned into the inside of my eyelids. Forcing my way through the packed space, I eventually stop at a safe distance to watch the aftermath of my unwelcome interruption. My satisfied smirk is wider than ever when I see Shiloh's *friend* turn a deep shade of scarlet while she laughs at his sodden pants.

Good. Serves him right for touching what doesn't belong to him.

The victory turns out to be better than I expected when my target ultimately chooses to leave the bar altogether. Unfortunately, Shiloh's expression doesn't betray even the slightest scrap of disappointment as she gives him a hasty hug and waves him out the door. It seems she doesn't care at all that her chances of an easy hookup have gone up in smoke, though the look on the guy's face once he's turned his back to her tells me that's exactly what he'd been hoping for.

My deep frown returns as I watch her merrily hand out new drinks to her friends before stumbling away from the bar like a newborn giraffe. For a split second I tense, initially assuming she's about to follow that douchebag out the door. My rigid spine relaxes as she veers towards the restrooms instead, bouncing off several disgruntled patrons as she fails to move her feet in a straight line.

Of course, this seems like a fine opportunity to stride after her, now that she's finally alone. I don't even know what I intend to say to her as I trace her footsteps through the crowd. Tell her I heard all the vicious shit she was spewing about me when she got here? Mock her for being so embarrassingly drunk?

Fuck knows.

I just want to smack that dazed smile off her face and

remind her of the hundred and one reasons I had to be angry at the world when we were kids.

But, as she throws out her hand to catch herself on the wall before she tips sideways once again, I realize that embarking on my own tirade right now would be a total waste of breath. She's too far gone to fuck with tonight. What would be the point in toying with prey that's barely conscious to start with?

Before I get close enough for her to notice she has company outside the restrooms, I spin on my heel and head straight for the door.

As soon as I make it halfway down the street, I rip the stupid mask off my face and take a deep breath of blissfully cool air. One more second trapped inside that rubbery sack of sweat and I may have clawed my own skin off just to feel freedom again.

"What the hell am I doing?" I grunt, running my hand over my face.

I'm more than ready to march straight to my car and break every speed limit until I'm back in my own State, but something stops me in my tracks. This pulsing adrenaline in my veins has made me feel more alive today than I have all year. I couldn't say if it's the thrill of being so close to my little Shy Girl without her having any idea who haunts her every step, or maybe the rush of power I felt crushing her hopes so easily this afternoon. Whatever it is, the prospect of leaving it behind just to go back to the same old grind of my life under my father's boot has my fingers curling into fists by my sides.

I *want* to stay.

Besides, I promised myself a break. And I've barely had

any fun here at all. What vacation is complete without a few leisurely activities?

The possibilities flit through my head one by one as my feet carry me back to my car. Another half hour or so passes in a haze of barely contained impatience. I watch Shiloh's house from where I lean in the shadows, until she finally appears, weaving unsteadily down the sidewalk. My lip curls in disgust at her childish antics, but I can't say I'm surprised. If I lived in this godforsaken corner of wasteland, I too would have to drink myself into a stupor just to make it through the day. I keep to the darkest parts of the street as I edge closer to her front yard, all the while she's fumbling with her keys as if her fingers are made of butter.

With a triumphant *"Aha!"* she finally manages to unlock the door, not bothering to switch on a light before stumbling inside. I linger behind a tree until I see a window illuminated on the upper floor, and then I make my approach.

Just as I suspected, she left the door unlocked. Whether she's too drunk to have remembered basic home security, or whether she thinks Avalon is a safe enough town to not have to consider these things, I don't care. All that matters is how infinitely easier it makes it for me to slip inside unnoticed.

My eyes take only seconds to adjust to the gloom before I'm moving through the hallway and deeper into the house I've never been invited to. It's quaint. *Cozy*, even, in a way that makes my skin crawl. Mismatched furniture crowds the tiny living room, and every available surface is crammed with piles of books, knick-knacks, and framed photos. My eyes are immediately drawn to one in particular–our parents, my mom and her dad, smiling ear to ear while their arms are curled around the shoulders of two young children.

Replacements, I think to myself bitterly. Another son and daughter they chose to have once Shiloh and I were both out of the house. No doubt, because the children they already had were unpleasant reminders of the lives they hated so much before they fell into bed with each other.

The sound of running water snaps me back to the present, and I forget all about the sour resentment churning in my stomach. It seems Shiloh has managed to drag herself into the shower, leaving me free to investigate upstairs without being discovered.

Grateful for the distraction, I sneak up the stairs, following the racket Shiloh is making as she warbles some off-key version of a Fleetwood Mac tune. There's only one door off the landing, telling me that Shiloh's bathroom is an ensuite.

Perfect. That means I can slip into her bedroom without worrying that she'll exit the bathroom behind me and cut off my escape.

Not that I'm not very adept at hiding when I need to.

I push open the door slowly, greeted by a thin mist hanging in the air as steam billows from a cracked door in the wall to my left. Shiloh's ear-splitting concert of one continues behind that door, a convenient indicator that it's safe to continue exploring. I don't even know what I'm looking for. Some insight into her life, perhaps. I can't figure out how best to fuck with her when I no longer know anything about her. Eleven years of separation has turned us into complete strangers.

If my brief, for-fun haunting of Avalon is going to have a lingering effect on Shy Girl, I need to get inside her mind.

My fingers trail across her dresser, brushing over more

books and cluttered possessions as I scan the room. We clearly couldn't be more opposite, she and I. My apartment back in the city is an ode to stark minimalism, as crowded rooms make me feel suffocated.

Shiloh, on the other hand, apparently spends her meager salary on all manner of pointless collectibles. Tiny ornaments in the shapes of mushrooms and pumpkins and frogs, alongside dishes of tangled jewelry, are strewn across every available surface. Careful not to nudge anything out of place, I yank open a drawer, raising an eyebrow at the explosion of haphazard lace and cotton that greets me.

Clearly not in my right mind, I start tossing the contents onto the bed behind me, rifling through it all in search of fuck knows what. Some sneering voice in the back of my head tells me Shiloh could be exactly the kind of pathetic excuse for a human who would keep a journal. That would truly be the jackpot–a window straight into her fragile little soul.

I scour the rest of the room, growing increasingly frustrated as I come up empty-handed. If my little Shy Girl does spill her innermost thoughts onto paper, she doesn't keep the evidence in this room.

"Players only *love you* when they're playing," Shiloh's voice crescendos in the shower, her ghastly rendition of *Dreams* reaching its climax. I can't tell how long this impromptu performance is going to last. I'm already pushing my luck by daring to hang around while nothing more than a slightly ajar door separates the two of us. But as I turn to go, my gaze catches on the scattered underwear I've left on top of her sheets. Almost against my own will, I find myself reaching out, fingers ghosting over the delicate fabric.

I lift a scrap of black lace, an image swirling into sharp focus of Shiloh peeling the thong down her silky, pale legs. Heat rushes through me, a confused mix of desire and revulsion. I drop the underwear like it's coated in acid, stumbling back from the bed.

The shower squeaks off abruptly, the sudden silence yanking me out of my daze. Cursing under my breath, I dart for the door, pausing only for a split second to sweep my gaze over the room one last time. A monument to my absolute failure to be discreet, Shiloh's bedroom is a mess. Drawers hang open, ornaments have been tipped on their sides, an embarrassing contrast to my usual ruthless precision.

Fuck it. Let her wonder what the hell happened here. Let her feel just as unsettled as I do right now.

I hurry from the room and down the stairs before Shiloh emerges from her bathroom, her resumed humming suggesting that she's taking her sweet ass time getting ready for bed. The cool night air hits me like a slap this time, clearing some of the fog from my head. I stalk towards my car, feeling uncomfortably rattled.

This *won't* do. I say I'm sticking around with the sole intention of messing with Shiloh's peace. So why the fuck do I feel like my own composure is already cracking apart?

5

SHILOH

I STEP out of the bathroom, grateful to be a little steadier on my feet. Lord knows it would be just my luck to drunkenly slip in the shower and meet an early death just when I started feeling a little better about existing. However, I freeze mid-stride, my breath catching in my throat as the slightly blurry scene in my bedroom suddenly comes into focus.

Most of the underwear I own is strewn across my bed, various drawers hang half open, and the usually organized chaos of my surfaces appear in an unfamiliar disarray. Blood pounds in my ears as I slowly creep forward, my fingers trembling when I reach out to pick up a pair of lace panties.

Real. This is real. I'm not drunkenly hallucinating right now.

"What the fuck?" I mutter to myself, before calling out louder. "Hello? Is anyone there?" My voice cracks a little on the final question. Nothing but silence answers me, of course. I don't know why I would expect an intruder to announce themselves like a fucking amateur. The apparent stillness throughout the house does nothing to quell the panic in my chest. I head to my closet, throwing open the doors and pushing the hangers aside in one anxious swipe.

Empty.

I drop to my knees next, peering under the bed in search of a lurking monster. I find nothing there besides dust bunnies and a lone sock. With a relieved sort of huff, I clamber to my feet again, my gaze snapping to the windows. Both locked, just as I left them.

Only when I've stood in silence for a solid five minutes, ears straining for any sound throughout the rest of the house, does the hammering within my ribcage begin to slow. I close my eyes on a deep inhale, trying to piece together the fuzzy memories of when I got home. Just seconds later, I'm forced to peel them back open again, the Earth seeming to tilt while an ungodly volume of alcohol still flows through my veins.

"Oh fuck," I sputter, throwing my arms out to steady the violent swaying. A slightly hysterical laugh bursts from my lips as I take in the carnage of my upturned bedroom again. "I must be way more drunk than I thought."

Assuming I'm the culprit for creating such a mess in a wasted haze, I wordlessly curse myself as I go about tidying everything back into its right place. With each item I put away, the anxious knot in my stomach loosens a bit.

By the time I climb into bed, a heavy exhaustion has settled deep in my bones, though my mind is still relentlessly spinning. I pull the covers up to my chin, fighting back the nausea that threatens an entirely different kind of mess. Clearly not about to fall asleep any time soon, I reach across to my nightstand and grab my phone. Before I even realize what I'm doing, my fingers move on autopilot, typing in my code and pulling up Instagram.

It only takes a couple more clicks before Dominic's profile fills the screen, a window into a world so far removed from mine, it might as well be on another planet. I scroll, transfixed, each passing image a carefully curated glimpse into a life of luxury.

Here I am on a yacht, the Mediterranean sparkling behind me.

Here I am at some glitzy event, surrounded by women who probably model for Vogue.

Here's the view from my fancy-shmancy corner office where lowly failures aren't permitted to tread.

Every photo is a cutting reminder of the vast chasm between us, of everything he prioritizes over his own family–over the life he could've had in Avalon if he didn't consider us all so far beneath him. I stop furiously scrolling when the bitter resentment starts to taste a little too much like rising bile. My thumb is left hovering over a picture of Dom in a tailored suit, leaning against a sleek sports car. The corner of his mouth is lifted in that infuriating smirk he seems to wear all too well.

"*Ugh*," I groan, tossing my phone aside. I grab my pillow and slam it over my head, as if I might be able to smother the rage he evokes from me.

But in the darkness behind my eyelids, I can't escape the images that flow past in a taunting carousel. Dominic's life of glamor and excess, so starkly contrasted with my own modest existence. It's not even that I'm jealous of the money and the success. *I'm not.* I know damn well that I could do whatever I wanted with my life if I chose to leave Avalon.

I *chose* to stay, pathetically clinging to a futile dream that my family would one day appreciate me for choosing them. And yet, it seems like the more years I spend trying to stay close to them, the further they drift away.

My dad and Dom's mom, Vivienne, had two more kids after I left for college, and now all their time is spent raising their second-chance family. I consider it a luxury if they even ask to have dinner together on my birthday.

And then there's Dominic, willfully tossing away everything I crave as if it means nothing. He was supposed to understand me. He was supposed to care about clawing back some kind of family from the carnage of both our parents' broken marriages. But he cares as little as they do, not bothering to stick around and be the comforting presence I'd always hoped he'd grow into when we were younger. A protective older brother, or a like-minded best friend, who knows what I wanted from him...

Fact is, he doesn't give a shit.

I throw the pillow back off my face, dangerously close to smothering myself if I'd clung to it much longer. As I lie here, panting slightly, the sounds of the present grow muffled and indistinct. Instead, I hear the jarring slam of a door, the eerie creek of old floorboards under encroaching footsteps.

The memory swims in front of my open eyes before I can shove it back in a box I usually keep firmly locked, as vivid as if it were happening all over again...

I'm curled up on our worn sofa, blissfully lost in the pages of my latest obsession–a dog-eared copy of Wuthering Heights. *The house is quiet, and my parents have long since left for their usual Friday night dinner. I've just reached the chapter where the myste-*

rious Heathcliff returns after a long absence, when the front door swings open and clatters against the hallway wall.

I almost leap out of my skin before Dominic appears in the living room doorway, his presence seeping into my peace like a gathering storm cloud. He leans against the jamb, arms crossed, that infuriating smirk playing at his full lips.

"Another fun-filled Friday night for the bookish loner, huh?" he drawls, eyeing me with piercing disdain I've grown so accustomed to over the years.

"Leave me alone, Dom," I grumble, rolling my eyes before lowering them again, determined to focus on my novel and not my asshole stepbrother.

He ignores my dismissal, of course, pushing off the doorframe and stepping closer. "Aw, don't be like that, Shy Girl. I'm just concerned about your glaring lack of a social life. It's not normal for a girl to be so isolated at fifteen. You should be having sleepovers and practicing kissing with your girly friends."

My fingers tighten on the edges of my book, my jaw clenching as I try desperately to ignore him. "I said, leave me alone."

"You know," Dom continues, as if I hadn't spoken at all, "if you won't leave the house of your own accord..." He trails off, disappearing into the hallway and leaving me with the creeping feeling that he's not even close to being done. When he reappears only seconds later, that feeling turns to ice in my veins.

In his hands is my dad's baseball bat, the one he leaves by the door as if he expects to one day use it on an intruder. Dom smacks the wood against his palm a couple of times, the harsh slap ringing out in the suddenly too-quiet room. His eyes, dark and menacing, lock onto mine.

"... maybe you need some motivation."

"Dom... n-not now. I d-don't want to."

He simply sneers, his voice dropping to a threatening whisper when he simply answers, "I'll give you a thirty second head start."

For the span of a single heartbeat, I'm rooted in place. Then, familiar adrenaline floods my system and I'm moving. I vault over the back of the sofa, my forgotten book tumbling to the floor. Dom's laughter booms behind me as I sprint through the house, my bare feet slapping almost painfully against the floorboards.

I burst through the back door, silently praying that he'll deem this a worthy example of leaving the house and leave me be. Of course, I'm hoping in vain. I can already hear Dom behind me, his longer strides eating up the distance between us as I race across the backyard.

The fence looms ahead and I push myself harder, gritting my teeth against the bite of the cold ground beneath my feet. I leap, my fingers barely scraping the rough wood before I'm stumbling on the other side. The woods that border our small patch of land rush up to meet me, my only hope of maybe finding somewhere to hide. I throw myself into the dense tangle of trees and shadows without hesitation, branches whipping at my face and arms as I run.

My lungs burn, a heady blend of fear and exhaustion making each breath a battle of pure will. Dom's footsteps are getting closer. I risk a glance over my shoulder and instantly regret it.

He's right there.

I turn back with a whimper, narrowly avoiding colliding head-first with a tree. But the slip costs me the last of my head start. Dom tackles me from behind, dragging me to the ground in a tangle of limbs. He flips me onto my back, pinning my arms above my head as sharp twigs and rocks stab into my skin.

I can only glare up at him, my chest heaving as I try and gulp down the oxygen I need to stay conscious. He looms over me, a predatory, almost maniacal grin splitting his face. And his eyes...

those dark pits seem to burn with something I can't name, something that sends a thrill dancing along the edges of my fear.

"Better luck next time, Shy Girl," he taunts me, digging his knees into my ribs just to demonstrate how helplessly he has me pinned. For a moment, we stay like that, the only sound our ragged breaths and the crunch of the forest floor beneath us.

And then, all at once, the game is over. The thrill seems to die in Dom's eyes, reducing them again to hardened onyx. He pushes himself to his feet, sparing me one last mocking glance before turning and striding back to the house as if nothing had happened.

I don't know how long I stay there, staring at the tree canopy. Only when my heart has relaxed to a normal pace, and the chill of the ground beneath my thin T-shirt becomes too painful to bear, do I haul myself up and trudge back the same way on aching feet.

I snap back to the present with a jolt. My hands fly to my cheeks, feeling a traitorous heat blooming there. My heart is racing, and I'm not sure if it's the lingering memory or... something else entirely.

Huffing a frustrated sigh, I lean over and flick off my bedside lamp. The darkness settles over me like a heavy weight that feels more ominous than comforting. Rest eludes me. Despite the alcohol, I toss and turn and tangle myself in the sheets.

When sleep finally does seize me, I dream of running through dark woods. The vision warps and remakes itself over and over again. Sometimes it's the memory of Dom chasing me, our old Run and Hide game in full swing. Sometimes I'm the one pursuing him. And others, we're fleeing together from some faceless threat.

But always, *always*, it ends with us tangled together on the forest floor, Dom's dark eyes boring into mine, my breath catching in my throat.

I wake with the dawn, a deathly headache pounding behind my eyes. I'm lost in a haze as a ghastly hangover pins me down–rather than the shadow of my stepbrother.

6

DOMINIC

I WAKE to the scent of stale lavender and mothballs. Blinking away the lingering weight of a restless night's sleep, the hideous floral wallpaper of my room swims into focus.

Ugh, waking up in this B&B feels like being throttled with my dead grandmother's wardrobe.

I groan at the assault on my senses, swinging my legs over the edge of the bed and rubbing the crusting of sleep from my tear ducts. The ancient springs beneath me creak in protest, urging me to leap to my feet before the whole thing collapses.

I guess that's one way to force someone out of bed.

I shower and dress quickly, the walls feeling like they're closing in on me with every second I spend trapped in this hellhole. "Some fucking vacation," I mutter to myself. I'm just about ready to march out the door with no real plan for how to spend my day when my phone starts buzzing in my pocket.

The moment I catch sight of the name on the screen, I consider hurling the whole damn thing out the window.

Instead, I bite back a string of foul curse words and swipe to answer. "Hello, Mother."

"Dom, darling! I just heard the most interesting news," her shrill voice chirps merrily through the speaker. "Apparently, you were spotted leaving the coffee house yesterday. Why didn't you tell me you were coming to visit us after all this time?"

I pinch the bridge of my nose hard enough to risk a bruise, focusing on the pain to anchor me before I lose my mind. "I'm not here for a social visit. Just some quick business and then I'm leaving."

"Nonsense," she tuts. "You have to come and have Sunday brunch with us at least. The whole family together, doesn't that sound lovely?"

"No," I snap, picturing her jumping slightly at my harsh tone. "I don't have time."

"But Dom–"

"I gotta go. We'll speak another time." I hang up before she can protest. Tossing the phone onto the bed, I claw my hand through my hair, my gaze wandering to the view from my window. Main Street stretches out before me, a fucking Norman Rockwell painting brought to life. Ancient little shops, tree-lined sidewalks, and a bunch of irritating gossip mongers who can't help but report everything and everyone they see as if it's breaking news.

Clearly, I won't be able to go anywhere in this town without someone reporting it to my mother. The obvious move would be to leave now, and head back to the city where I belong. I should give up on this failure of a *fun vacation*. I can't torment Shiloh and avoid the rest of my family at the same time.

Shame. I'd felt like the rush of yesterday's antics was just the tip of the iceberg, once I had calmed down. And I didn't even get to see whether or not Shiloh seemed shaken after my little visit...

"Fuck it," I sigh, grabbing my leather gloves and storming out the door.

Thirty minutes and a brief text to my mother later, I'm pulling into the parking lot of Old Mabel's Diner. I kill the engine but can't quite bring myself to move just yet, gripping the steering wheel until my gloves creak.

Am I really going to go through with this just for the chance to stay in town a little longer without being hassled?

It seems the answer is '*yes*' as I slam the car door shut and stride into the lion's den.

The nauseating smell of cheap coffee and maple syrup hit me like a thick tsunami, and I almost turn right back around– which seems to be a growing habit of mine. The only thing that stops me is an enthusiastic wave from the mother who's unfortunately already spotted me. She has a megawatt smile plastered on her face as she swings her arm through the air with such gusto it might just fall off. Next to her my stepfather, Charlie, offers a tentative nod. Finally, bouncing in their seats like caffeinated chimp-babies are Theo and Ellen–the replacement spawn.

Here we all are, the happy little family plus one black sheep.

I approach slowly, still considering leaving, each step feeling like I'm wading through the very syrup this place reeks of. My mother leaps out of her seat as I finally reach the table, arms thrown wide.

"Oh, Dom! So glad you made it!" She envelops me in a cloud of floral perfume and latent maternal affection. I stand there stiffly until she lets go. "Let me look at you. My goodness, you've packed on some muscle! Do you ever leave the gym?"

"Yes, Mother. Oddly enough I have a job to go to, if you remember." I roll my eyes with enough dismissal to have her stepping back, her bright expression faltering slightly. Charlie extends his hand next to her.

"Dom. Good to see you." The strain in his voice is almost enjoyable, as he's clearly as thrilled about this gathering as I am. Can't say Shiloh was the only one I indulged in tormenting as a kid.

"Charlie." I respond, briefly shaking his hand with my firmest grip. His wince has the corner of my mouth curling up.

Theo and Ellen are practically vibrating out of their skin with excitement. We've never met, but it seems they've built up some story in their mind that I'm going to be a doting older brother. I can't wait to crush that dream in my fist.

"Dom! Dom! Guess what?" Theo yells, waving his arms in the air like the spitting image of our mother.

"Indoor voice, sweetie," she chides gently.

I slide into the chair across from him. "What?" I ask, not one trace of interest coloring my tone.

"I lost another tooth yesterday!" Theo grins wide, proudly showing off the gap in the center of his mouth.

"And then! And *then!* A FAIRY came!" Ellen pipes up, determined to not let her older brother hog the spotlight.

"For real! I got a whole five dollars!" Theo tacks on.

"Wow," I deadpan. "Inflation really is hitting everyone these days."

Charlie clears his throat, attempting to make it sound like

a lighthearted chuckle. "So, Dom. How's the Big Apple treating you? Still climbing the old corporate ladder?"

I lean back, crossing my arms over the overcoat I haven't bothered to remove. "There's not much left to climb, unless I decide to murder my own father."

My mother jumps in, immediately sensing the danger of an awkward silence. "Oh, but surely you want a break from working so hard all the time. How long are you staying? We'd love to have you over for dinner, you haven't been in town for a decade. Doesn't that sound insane? A *decade*, for goodness' sake."

"I'm not sure yet," I hedge. "Depends how my business works out."

"Well, you simply have to make time to see us all again before you leave," she insists. "Have you even told Shiloh you're here?"

At the mention of my sister, my fingers clench involuntarily. "She knows."

"Oh, you've spoken to her? How is she? We haven't caught up in ages, these two little ones keep us busy beyond belief. Is everything good with her?"

I arch an eyebrow, stunned that *I* should be the one around this table being asked about Shiloh's wellbeing. Our parents live barely five miles from their eldest daughter, but apparently that's too much of a distance to keep tabs on her life. "She's a little stressed actually. That ridiculous Halloween Ball-thing lost its sponsor and now she's nervous her school is gonna miss out on funding."

"Damn," Charlie sighs. "That place is so important to her. And she adores the Ball, she must be devastated."

I snort. "Yeah, she seemed really cut up about it when she called to beg me for the cash."

The table falls silent again, Charlie's brows lowering in a deep frown. "Shiloh asked you for money?"

"Sure did. She was clearly hoping for a bailout from her dear, long-lost brother. I told her just where to stick her charity case."

My mother's eyes widen comically as Charlie's lips flatten into a grimace. "Dominic! That's your sister you're talking about."

"Step sister," I correct her automatically. "If you can even call her that. We're practically strangers to each other. She may as well have called any random dude on Wall Street for a handout."

The pair of them just gape at me for a moment, as if I'd just told them I was on a mission to bring Hitler back from the dead. The tension is broken by Ellen tugging impatiently on my mother's sleeve. "Mommy, is Shiloh coming for pancakes too?"

"I hope so, my love," Mother simpers. "I think she's just running a little late."

Right on cue, that infernal bell above the door chimes again. I glance up and there she is. Shiloh stands frozen in the doorway, her wide eyes locked on our charming little gathering.

Well, this should be interesting.

Shiloh's expression slowly morphs from shock to something harder, more guarded, as she approaches our table with measured steps.

"Well, isn't this a surprise?" she says as she reaches the

chair beside mine, her greeting dripping with false cheer. "The prodigal son returns."

My mother beams, apparently determined to ignore the thick tension. "Shiloh, my love. We were just talking about you."

Shiloh slides into the chair beside mine, scraping it across the floor in her effort to leave a wide berth between us. "Hey Viv, hey dad," she says warmly before turning to the kids. "Hey there, little munchkins, what's crackalackin'?"

Theo and Ellen launch immediately into excited chatter about anything and everything they can think of to say to the older sister they seem to see almost as little as I do. I watch in silence as Shiloh nods enthusiastically, playing the role of the big sister perfectly as she peppers the conversation with the appropriate *oh, cool*'s and *no way*'s.

It grates on my nerves to no end.

"So," I interject when there's finally a blissful lull. "Nice of you to grace us with your presence. I would think you'd be too busy with planning the costume party of the century, or whatever."

Or wasting away in bed with a raging hangover.

Shiloh narrows her eyes at me, all warmth bleeding from her expression like I'd stabbed her in the face. "I always show up for my family. Unlike some people who'd rather pretend we don't exist."

My mother titters nervously and shifts in her seat. "Now, you two. Please, let's not bicker. It's once in a blue moon that we all get to be together like this."

Charlie nods, obviously eager to provide backup to the peacekeeping mission. "Your mother's right. How about we order some grub? I know two little gremlins who are dying for some pancakes."

But the damage is already done. Shiloh and I stare daggers at each other. The façade of happy families well and truly shatter on the floor, years of festering resentment spilling out.

"Dear me, Shy Girl. I know you're really put out about this whole ball thing, but there's no need to bring such a negative attitude to brunch. Are you feeling well?" I smirk at her, gleefully leaching out every last ounce of fury I can.

"Me?" she whisper yells. "No one fucking wants you here, Dom. Why don't you do us all a favor and drag *your* shitty attitude back across state lines where it belongs?"

"Language, Shiloh!" my mother gasps. But that's all she says. No disagreement. No blubbering speech about how she's desperate for her first-born to stay right here. It seems the limits of her stunned joy have been reached, and now she's remembering how difficult I made life for all of them when I *was* here all the time.

Another second of tense silence and something in me snaps. I spring to my feet, nearly upending the table in the process. The rest of the diner has fallen eerily still, all eyes seemingly glued on our familial spat.

"You'd like that wouldn't you?" I growl at my brave little step sister, yanking my wallet from my pocket. I pull out a wad of cash—easily a few hundred dollars—and drop it on the table with a satisfying slap. "Here. Consider this my contribution to our happy family fun time."

Without waiting for a response, I spin on my heel and storm back out the door, my gloved hands clenched into fists.

Who the hell does she think she is, dismissing me like she has the high ground? As if she's better than me for hanging around this backwater town for a family who couldn't give two shits about her.

Fury causes my vision to blur. Over my dead fucking body, will Shiloh get to dictate what I do. If she wants me out of town, so she can go back to begging for scraps of our parents' hard-won attention, then she can damn well have the opposite.

I'm here to fucking *break* her now.

Good luck getting rid of me, Shy Girl.

You have no idea what's coming to you.

7

SHILOH

Okay, seriously, that is not where I left my fucking notebook.

It's entirely possible I may be losing my mind. Either that, or I've somehow attracted a poltergeist. Every minute I spend at home, I feel that prickly feeling on the back of my neck like someone's watching me. And whenever I move from one room to another, I get the sense that things are out of place.

Not disordered enough to make me think I've been robbed, or that a messy little raccoon has taken up residence in some secret hiding spot. Just enough to convince me I'm losing my damn marbles whenever I find something on a different shelf to where I was sure I had left it.

The stress of life is clearly getting to me and we're barely a month into the fall semester.

One saving grace of this week so far is that I haven't laid eyes on Dominic since our disastrous run-in at Sunday brunch. If I've earned myself any good fortune at all, he'll stay hundreds of miles away for another ten years.

Hell, forever would also work for me.

I stuff my notebook into my backpack and rush out the door for another Friday committee meeting. As much as I doubt we can depend on her for anything, I find myself praying that Melanie has come up with some miraculous solution to our funding problem. Lord knows my attempt to save us all went up in black flames.

Trying my hardest to banish all thoughts of the shitshow that was Dominic's brief visit, I push through the heavy wooden doors of the town hall and make my way to the conference room. The eerie silence that greets me as I reach the final corridor, has my eyebrows knitting together.

Has the meeting been canceled? Surely someone would have let me know if we'd called quits on the whole doomed affair?

As the door swings open, my entire world tilts on its axis, and I find myself wishing that a canceled Halloween Ball was the full extent of my problems.

There, sitting at the head of the table like he owns the fucking place, is my one and only stepbrother. He bares all his teeth in a wicked grin as our eyes meet, my stomach dropping to my feet like a lead ball. I find myself wondering what I could have possibly done in a past life to deserve this torment. My mouth has gone completely dry, my tongue reduced to a useless lump, incapable of forming any of the burning questions I'm dying to spit at the smug Dominic.

"Shiloh, there you are! You're the last to arrive," Melanie's pointed barb cuts through my stunned paralysis. "Sit yourself down then and we can get started."

I clench my jaw and force my legs to move, practically falling into the nearest empty chair. Jemma purses her lips in obvious concern opposite me, her eyes dropping to where my fists tremble on the tabletop. I shove them in my lap as Melanie claps her hands together, clearly for lack of a damn gavel.

"Alright everybody, I guess I'll jump right in and introduce the newest member of our group!" Her eyes are gleaming with barely contained glee, fixed on me in a way that infinitely deepens my sense of dread. Whatever's coming, I know I'm not going to like it. "Please give a warm welcome to Mr. Dominic Blackwood, one of our very own Avalon High alumnae. After a little wooing from yours truly, he has generously offered to sponsor this year's Halloween Ball."

A chorus of relieved sighs and excited murmurs erupts around the table. But me? I feel like I've just been punched in the gut.

"Not *only* that, but he's also pledged to match all donations made to the school during the event itself! Isn't that incredible? Such a lucky turn of events that I ran into him at the market earlier this week and managed to recruit him to our cause."

This is some kind of surreal nightmare, involving a massive spider web and a pair of fanged predators. How is it possible that I'm being pinned by the self-satisfied smirks of Melanie *and* Dominic at the same time? The sensation feels like I'm physically trapped in a sticky cocoon, unable to wriggle free and slowly suffocating.

This is hell. I'm in hell.

"I'm sure we're all thrilled to have such a dedicated and committed sponsor as Mr. Blackwood, especially seeing as he's insisted on lending a helping hand to our committee, on top of bankrolling the whole thing. He'll be working closely with Shiloh to help her organize the venue decoration, and I'm sure they'll make a great team."

My eyebrows almost disappear into my hairline this time. Sparing an agonized glance at Jemma, I can see that hers have done the same. Of course, no one else in the room is aware of just how screwed up the arrangement is. Other than Dominic, who's smug stare is still fixated on me.

I force myself to focus on Melanie as she dives into outlines of everyone else's current responsibilities in the run up to Halloween. I can't even hear what she's saying, because my mind is nothing but a haze of confusion.

What the hell is his angle with all this?

Once the meeting wraps up, several committee members rush to crowd around Dominic, showering him with praise and profuse thanks. He lets it all wash over him with a distinctly bored expression, evidently not sharing Melanie's craving to be worshiped. The more I watch him, the less sense it makes. I can't pinpoint any rational motivation that would keep him in town at all, let alone volunteering to throw the same Ball he so viciously mocked to my face.

"What's he playing at?" Jemma murmurs as she catches me by the door. "The guy gives me the creeps."

"Hell if I fucking know," I mutter back, desperate to leave the room before I explode.

I make it as far as the parking lot before he's caught up to me. "Well, partner," he drawls, "looks like you and I have lots to be getting on with."

The urge to scratch his eyes out is so strong, I have to dig my nails into my palms just to sheath them. "If you sabotage this event as part of some sick game, I swear to God, I'll stab you and toss you in a ditch," I spit, rounding on him as I reach the sidewalk.

That infernal smirk doesn't falter for a second. "Now, now. Is that any way to thank your generous benefactor?"

"I would literally take *anyone* else at this point. Why are you doing this? Why won't you just leave me the fuck alone like you always have?"

"I thought you'd be pleased," he says with a mock-innocent shrug. "Isn't this what you wanted? Funding for your precious Halloween Ball...a chance to reconnect with your long-lost big bro. Where's all this hostility coming from? Most people would be grateful for such a generous offer."

"Most people don't have psychotic stepbrothers who get off on torturing them," I snap. "What's this really about, Dominic? Are so you bored with your own life, you have to come and fuck with mine?"

He raises a handsome dark eyebrow, looking me over like I've grown an extra head. "Bold of you to assume you occupy so much of my attention, Shy Girl. Wishful thinking on your part, perhaps."

I claw both my hands through my tangled hair with an outraged scoff. "Yeah, yeah. Make me sound like the crazy one, why don't you? Just like you always did. None of your issues are my fucking fault, so quit punishing me for them already!"

"I have no idea what you're talking about." He makes every word sound like its own sentence, forcing them through a clenched jaw.

"Yes, you do. You know exactly what I mean. Are you really going to stand here and pretend like you didn't take all your anger out on me when we were kids? As if I was the reason your mom chose to break up her own marriage? As if it was my fault she dragged you away from your precious city to live in this *backwater town?*"

His eyes flash menacingly as he steps closer to me, getting right in my face. "You think this is about any of that ancient history?"

"Isn't it always?" I jab viciously at his chest, though he doesn't yield an inch. But I don't care, I'm on a roll now, years of pent-up frustration pouring out of me. "I can't think of any other reason you'd be doing all this. You just want to shit all over my life because you can't stand to see me happy. You can't deal with the fact that I turned out okay and you're royally fucked up."

He laughs viciously, as he leans down, so close I can feel his breath. "Don't flatter yourself. I'm doing this for the same reason I do anything. Because I fucking *can*. Because it amuses me to watch you squirm. And if you're really so *okay,* so damn unshakeable, how is it that it's so easy to rattle you?"

My own body betrays me as warmth floods to my core, and I recoil slightly, disgust churning in my stomach. "You're sick, you know that?"

"And you're pathetic," Dominic sneers. "Still so desperate for approval, for someone to care. Newsflash, Shy Girl: *nobody cares.* Your own mother didn't care enough to stick around, our parents don't care enough to be part of your life even though they live minutes away, and I sure as fuck don't give a rat's ass. Face it, I just remind you of your own glaring insignificance."

Every word hits me like a physical blow, pummeling my skin until I'm certain it's black and blue beneath my clothes. I open my mouth to sling back a retort, but nothing comes out.

No, I'm *hurt.*

His look of satisfaction at my devastated silence is too much for me to bear any longer. I turn and run. Like we're teenagers all over again, I flee from him. Blinking back the sting of threatening tears the entire way, I sprint to my home, desperate to be alone. Desperate to lock myself away in the one place he can't get to me.

8

DOMINIC

MY FEET CARRY me down the sidewalk at a punishing pace, in the complete opposite direction of the one Shiloh ran off in. Each thunderous step I take pounds an echo of my stormy mood.

That got a little out of hand.

The image of Shiloh's face, flushed and defiant, is seared into my eyeballs, refusing to fade no matter how many times I blink. My ears still ring with the tremor in her voice as she tried so hard to stand up to me. Even as I shake with rage, I can't deny the thrill that hums in my veins–and the pang, albeit small, of *guilt* for making her cry.

Fuck me. Fuck this town. And fuck her.

An elderly couple strolling hand in hand practically dive out of my way as I march down the sidewalk, likely sensing the hostility rolling off me in waves.

"Watch where you're walking, Dominic Blackwood!" the woman shrieks at my back. I didn't spare them a glance to see who they were, but they obviously recognized me.

"Eat a dick, you old crone," I mutter, keeping my words hushed just to avoid another phone call from my mother.

The only justification I can conjure for being so furious at Shiloh is frustration at how utterly wrong she is. I've never resented her for my mother's affair, and never blamed her for the years I had to spend trapped here. What an absurd idea to think I held her responsible for the choices our parents made and forced us both to endure.

Truth is, the years have shown me just how much of a raging asshole my father can be. I knew it back then, but I know it better now. He drove my mother away with his fierce ambition and neglect. Nothing matters to him beyond money and power—not his wife and not his own fucking kid.

He didn't even care where *I* ended up, until the day he realized he needed time to mold his sole heir and demanded I return to the city. *"If you're not a shark in this world, you're a worm."* He used to tell me, over and over again until I learned to think and act like he does.

If I'm as fucked up as Shiloh claims, no doubt *he's* the one to blame.

And for the record, the reason I tortured my step sister so harshly when we were kids was because she made it too damn easy. The parts of my DNA I inherited from my father relished the power too much. Shiloh was always such a cowardly little mouse, letting everyone walk all over her in the hopes they'd love her for it.

It was so pathetic, I couldn't help myself. She was beneath me. They all are. I can't resist the sweet satisfaction of proving it time and again. Like today, Shiloh tried so hard to prove she's grown a backbone over the last eleven years, and it was too tempting to crush it.

No wonder I'm obsessed.

My mind flashes back to only moments before. Those bright blue eyes are stunning when they glisten with unshed tears. The way her lower lip trembles when she's fighting to hold herself together, it's sinfully delicious. And the slight catch in her breath when I leaned in close, invading her personal space? I could live on that shit for a hundred years.

I'd reduced her to a pretty little mess with nothing more than a few harsh words, and the power of it was the most intoxicating drug I've ever tasted. I want to do it again. I want to see how far I can make her bend before she breaks completely.

Fuck, I want destroy her.

The realization that my cock is rock hard in my tailored slacks hits me like a ton of bricks. For the first time, I'm grateful that I'm not walking the busy streets of Manhattan. The last thing I want is to be recognized sporting a raging hard-on in the middle of the sidewalk. I force myself to keep moving, trying to think of anything that will distract me from the ache inside my boxers. But it's hopeless, my mind just keeps circling back to Shiloh. To the way she crumbled right before my eyes. The way she ran from me just like she used to.

The B&B finally comes into view, and I almost groan with relief. I take the porch steps two at a time, surging through the foyer without sparing the waving owners a second glance. I just need the privacy of my room.

I slam the door behind me much harder than I intended. Breathing heavily, I lean against the chipped paint, my cock still painfully hard. The tension coiled in my gut is almost unbearable, tangled live wires of need and frustration. Still, I try to claw back control.

Pacing the room like a caged animal, I can only make it five steps in each direction before I have to turn around again. This shitty room is claustrophobic as fuck, nothing like my sprawling apartment back home. But right now, my whole world seems to have narrowed down to one singular focus, balanced on a knife edge.

Shiloh.

My fingers twitch with the overwhelming urge to touch her, to grab fistfuls of that blonde hair and yank her head back with all my strength. I want to trace the delicate skin of her throat and feel her erratic pulse flutter beneath my palm.

But all I can do instead is throw myself down on my bed in agonized frustration and pull out my phone. Just as I've done every night this week, I pull up her Instagram, my eyes devouring every image with a new hunger.

I scroll through each snapshot with rapt attention, though I've got every one memorized already. In one, she smiles in front of a gleaming whiteboard in her classroom. In another, she's beaming over the top of a precarious tower of books.

She looks so fucking innocent.

My dick throbs, and I groan again, giving into the inevitable. I slowly unzip my pants, yanking down my underwear until my erection springs free, flushed, leaking, and desperate for attention. I can't remember the last time I was this hard.

I wrap my hand around the shaft, hissing slightly at the rough scrape of my calloused palm. But I'm too impatient to seek out any kind of lube. Instead, I close my eyes and imagine it's Shiloh touching me. I can damn near feel the slight scrape of her teeth as she takes me in her mouth, staring up at me with those crystalline eyes. In my mind, I fist her hair, force her to take me deeper until she gags.

"That's it, Shy Girl," I mutter to myself, pumping my fist faster. "You can take it all for me."

All at once the fantasy shifts. Now she's bent over my desk in my office, her skirt hiked up around her waist while I fuck her in front of walls of towering windows. I spank her delicious ass until it's as red as her cheeks get when she blushes, then pound into her hard enough to leave bruises on her hips.

I'm close in no time, teetering on the edge as my hips start to buck off the mattress. My eyes snap back open as I lift my phone again off my chest. I scroll frantically through her feed again until I find exactly what I'm looking for. A portrait of Shiloh wearing a sundress, smiling timidly at the camera. It's so wholesome, so sweet–everything I'm hungry to corrupt.

I want to see those lips swollen and bruised after I've devoured them. I want to see that angelic face flushed and sweaty and smeared with my load. What is it about perfection that makes it so tempting to destroy?

I've always been this way. I see something delicate, and I want to break it. Watch the shards crumble at my feet, a new kind of beauty in their splintered remains. No other man could break Shiloh the way I could. I know her desires, her fears. I'd know how to tear her apart and put her back together again.

I tighten my fist until it's almost painful, imagining how her wet little pussy would feel clenched around me. How she'd scream as I filled her up and left my marks on every inch of her pale skin.

"Fuck, Shy Girl." I hiss through my teeth as I come, spilling over my hand and shirt in hot spurts.

For a moment, there's nothing but blissful release. Then reality comes crashing back like a bulldozer, shattering the bubble of my secret indulgence. It leaves me feeling hollow, empty, as I stare at the ceiling.

When I can force myself to move again, I clean up mechanically, pointedly avoiding my reflection in the mirror until I'm dressed in a fresh shirt and slacks. Even then, I can't bring myself to admit the truth written all over my guilty face.

It's just like she said. I'm sick.

The problem is, with every minute I spend watching her, following her, sneaking into her house while she sleeps...I find myself caring less and less that it's all kinds of wrong.

She's an addiction. A habit I don't intend to kick just yet.

9

SHILOH

THE GLOSSY, black business card mocks me my entire way down the stairs, glaring from the center of my welcome mat like the fucking Eye of Sauron. Nobody should have to face such a harbinger of doom first thing on a Saturday morning.

I know exactly who it's from without having to pick it up, so I stubbornly choose to ignore it, veering around the banister and heading straight to the kitchen for my caffeine fix. And yet, even through the wall I feel like that dark omen is burning a hole in the side of my face. Only when I drain the final dregs from my coffee mug do I finally decide I can't avoid it any longer.

The cardstock is thick, embossed with chrome lettering for the contact details of the one and only Dominic Blackwood. I wonder if he has these made from the pulped egos of every poor soul who's ever had the misfortune of speaking to him.

I don't like that he knows where I live. I like even less that he would have had to open my front door sometime during the night in order to leave this little gift for me. It sure as hell wasn't there when I went to bed. And in all the time I've lived alone in Avalon, I've never worried much about locking my door while I'm in the house. Nobody does.

It might be time for me to start.

"Creepy ass gargoyle," I mutter to myself, fishing out my phone so that I can save his number to my contacts. No doubt he's hoping I chuck the card in the trash so that he can complain to Melanie about my reluctance to work together. It's crossed my mind a few times, but I refuse to be labeled as the difficult one. If he wants to stick his nose in my business, he better buckle up. I'll drag him around every last Halloween store and pumpkin patch until he's crying fake blood.

With a mocking snort, I type out a quick text.

> ME: MEETING WITH THE CARETAKER AT
> FAIRCHILD MANOR, WHICH IS WHERE THE BALL
> WILL BE. 2PM. BE THERE OR FUCK OFF BACK
> TO WHATEVER HOLE YOU CRAWLED OUT OF.

I hit send before I can talk myself out of it, and then immediately regret the whole thing. What if he actually shows up? What if he doesn't? At this point, I honestly can't say which outcome I dread more.

I go through the motions of my day painfully on edge, glancing over my shoulder periodically as if I expect to find Dominic creeping up behind me. Fortunately, I manage to leave the market with all the groceries I need without having my own *lucky* run-in with my stepbrother like Melanie did.

Not so, fortunately, I find myself checking my phone with embarrassing frequency.

Each time I see zero notifications waiting for me, I'm thrust into a violent battle between relief and fury. I *don't* want him to respond. I *don't* want him in my town anymore. But I also can't deny how incredibly irritating it is to know he went to all that trouble of butting into the committee and arranging our *partnership*, only to ghost me completely.

By the time I'm climbing into my car to head to Fairchild Manor, the fucker still hasn't text me back and I'm done letting it bother me. This is certainly the better outcome. I don't want him breathing down my neck and offering snide commentary while I design the entire Ball for the first time. I've wanted to be entrusted with this role ever since I started teaching at Avalon High. It deserves my full, undivided attention.

After slamming the door, perhaps a little harder than necessary, I gun the engine and head to the outskirts of town. The quiet drive gives me an opportunity to organize my thoughts, redirect them from Dominic and focus more on how best to bring Melanie's *'macabre masquerade but make it sexy'* vision to life. Can't say the theme is exactly inspiring, but I'll do my best. I can only hope that my stepbrother's money makes an appearance, even if his stupid, smug face never does.

As I pull up to the imposing wrought-iron gates of Fairchild Manor, I can't help but do a little nervous gulp. The place is a Goliath of Victorian Gothic architecture, all sharp angles and looming towers that seem to pierce the overcast sky. Even in broad daylight, it's pretty terrifying.

An absolutely perfect spot to host an annual Halloween Ball.

The place has always fascinated and frightened me in equal measure. Legend has it, this house was built on the site where several women were burned at the stake during Avalon's very own witch trials. Almost two hundred years had passed by the time the Fairchild's purchased the plot, but even so, rumors of strange happenings started before the family even moved into their newly built home. And now, more than a hundred and fifty years after that, townsfolk still whisper that the land is cursed.

I'm almost certain ninety-nine percent of those tales are spread just to keep tourism alive. But still, it's hard not to be a little creeped out when the house is devoid of hundreds of costumed partygoers. Aside from that one vibrant night a year, Fairchild Manor looms as a perpetual dare for brave teenagers and the occasional troop of ghost hunters.

I've never been on either list.

"You've got this, Shiloh," I mutter to myself. "It's just a house. Just a big, creepy, possibly haunted house on some possibly cursed land. No big deal. You'll be fine."

With one last compulsive glance at my phone, I clamber out of my car and make my way to the front door. The moment my finger touches the doorbell, I startle backward, nearly falling off the porch. The resounding gong of the damn button seems to echo for miles.

"Fuck a duck," I hiss, massaging the ache in the center of my chest where my heart is furiously hammering. I glance around to see if anyone else heard–or see my embarrassing reaction.

For what seems like a lifetime, there's no response. I'm just about ready to retreat back to my car when the door finally swings open with a slow and ominous creak. I brace myself for...

Well, I'm not entirely sure what.

Perhaps Lurch from the Addams Family, or some other

monstrous welcome party? What I'm not prepared for is the sheer eyesore that is the caretaker's eccentric ensemble.

"Well, well, what have we here? Another lost soul seeking refuge from the ghastly land of the living?"

The man standing before me looks like he raided an opera theater's wardrobe before robbing a cheap gaudy boutique for accessories. His wild gray hair sticks out in all directions, only partially contained by a velvet top hat that's seen better days. I notice, with no small amount of concern, that his curling leather shoes appear to be on the wrong feet.

"Um, hi, Mr. Prescott? I'm Shiloh Wilson, we spoke on the phone." He stares down at my offered hand as if I've presented him with a dead fish, so I slowly withdraw it again, trying not to let my rising nerves drive me straight off the property. "I'm here about the Halloween Ball?"

"Ah, yes, of course! The grand spectacle of All Hallows' Eve!" He claps his hands together, a cacophony of clinking rings assaulting my eardrums. "Where are my manners? Cornelius Prescott, at your service." The strange man throws himself forward in a bow so low I'm worried he might crack his head on the floorboards.

"Thank you for taking the time to show me around today, Mr. Prescott. I can't wait to get started planning our event." It takes no small amount of effort to keep from laughing incredulously in the guy's face, but I have to give him kudos, he's obviously committed to his role as the weird caretaker in the haunted house.

"Yes, yes, a marvel it will be, indeed. But before we proceed, I simply must cleanse your aura. Can't have any negative energies mucking up the place, can we?"

Before I can even think of a coherent response to that

madness, he's producing a bundle of garden sage from...*somewhere*...and clicking open an old zippo lighter. I try not to cough violently as the pungent smoke fills my nose. Cornelius immediately gets to work, waving the burning herbs around me in an elaborate choreography I'd liken to the mating dance of some tropical bird.

"Tell me, Miss Wilson, have you any malevolent spirits attached to you at the present time? Any phantoms we may need to exorcise before I invite you to enter these hallowed halls?"

"N-none that I know of," I splutter, silently questioning whether dickbag stepbrothers count.

"Wonderful! We shouldn't have any reason to think our hosts will be disturbed by your presence then!" He ushers me inside with a grand sweep of his arm, seemingly oblivious to just how disturbed *I* am by *his* presence. "Let us start with the grand tour, shall we? This old girl has so many wondrous stories to tell, you know. Why, just the other day, I was having tea with the ghost of *the* Prudence Fairchild in the conservatory, and let me tell you..."

I allow myself to zone out of Cornelius' no doubt well-rehearsed tour speech as we wander deeper into the slowly decaying manor. Instead, I indulge in the opportunity to explore parts of the house I've never seen before. We sweep through room after room, each dustier and more cluttered than the last. Cobwebs cling to crystal chandeliers, and faded portraits of stern-faced ancestors glare down at us from every wall. It almost makes me sad to see such a beautiful microcosm of history fall into such disrepair.

"May I ask, Mr. Prescott," I interrupt his current ramble about his latest séance with the Avalon witches. "Does the

Ball not bring in enough money each year to maintain the place a little better?"

"I'm afraid not, dear child," he answers wistfully. "Mayor Thornby insists he should be able to host the Ball here each year free of charge, seeing as the property belongs to the town."

"Figures," I mutter to myself, utterly unsurprised that Melanie's purse-pinching father has negotiated such an arrangement. "Is that why we only ever host the event in the ballroom? Because the rest of the house is crumbling down?"

"Indeed, indeed. She could certainly do with a bit of a facelift," Cornelius titters. "Though the crown jewel of the Fairchild Estate is certainly one ethereal place to throw a party!"

To demonstrate his point, he flings open an ornate set of double doors with a dramatic flourish and beckons me inside. With a few flicked switches, he bathes the cavernous ballroom in a golden glow that almost makes me sigh. The room is stunning, even despite the layers of dust and the slightly musty smell. Baroque moldings frame floor-to-ceiling windows that are draped in heavy scarlet satin, the rest of the wall space dominated by more imposing portraits and deep crimson wallpaper.

"It's certainly something," I breathe, my mind whirling with the slideshow of the various ways this incredible space has been decorated for Halloween Balls of the past. A heady excitement fills me when I remember that it's my turn to bring to life a vision of my own.

"Oh, isn't it just?" Cornelius beams. "Esmerelda Fairchild used to throw the most scandalous parties once upon a time. I like to convene with her each year to get her thoughts on how our illustrious Ball turns out. No pressure, but she is quite an opinionated spirit!"

"Well, then I hope not to disappoint her."

"Marvelous!" He claps his hands together once again. "Well, I'll give you a moment to acquaint yourself with the space and conjure a sparkling premonition for the décor. I myself have some pressing matters to attend to in the spirit realm. You know what they say, "The dead wait for no man!""

Thankfully, I don't have to conjure an appropriate response to that as he sweeps out of the room in a flurry of velvet and jangling jewelry. I allow myself a quiet chuckle, shaking my head at the bizarre fellow before getting back to the task at hand. I pull out my notebook and start jotting down a few ideas, wandering around the vast space as I brainstorm how to bring it to life in a way that isn't too corny.

I'm in the middle of sketching out a rough floor plan when I hear a soft creak from behind me. I freeze, pen poised in mid-air while I fight an internal battle over whether or not to turn around.

"Hello?" I manage to call out, the slight tremor in my voice echoing off the walls. "Cornelius?"

No response comes. I shrug it off, dismissing the noise as a regular occurrence in such an old house. Its bones must shift often.

But then I hear it again.

This time the sound is closer. The hairs on the back of my neck stand to attention as if commanded by some phantom General. I turn in a slow circle, my eyes scouring every nook and cranny for a possible lurking guest.

"Okay, you can come out now. Ha, ha, very funny."

But nothing but mocking silence answers me, yet again.

Letting out an exasperated sigh, I look back down at my notes, determined to finish up my work and get the fuck out of here. Though I'm sure I just have an overactive imagination, there's no part of me that's keen to hang around long enough to find out if Cornelius really does have a host of ghostly friends living within these walls.

But just as I'm scribbling down a few more notes, the chandelier above me flickers. My heart kicks into a canter, almost breaking free of my ribcage in the process.

Probably time to call it a day...I can always come back with Jemma another time.

I take a few steps back, more than ready to make a hasty exit when something flickers in my peripheral.

A ragged gasp slips between my lips as I catch sight of a dark figure hovering at the opposite end of the room, half-shrouded in shadows where the dim chandelier can't reach. Tall, imposing, draped in a black hooded robe that obscures any hint of a face. Before I can even process what I'm seeing, an almost maniacal giggle bursts from my lips.

"I didn't realize Cornelius employed costumed actors! Well done, you really got me. The flickering lights were a nice touch."

The figure doesn't answer. Instead, they raise an outstretched hand clad in a black leather glove. I watch with bated breath, intrigued to see where the performance might go next, because that is what *this* is...*right*? But when they start to move, rushing straight at me, my automatic fight-or-flight instinct kicks in.

"Nope!" I squeal, immediately spinning around to head straight for the door. I burst out of the ballroom, the sound of my thundering footsteps ricocheting throughout the empty hallway. A quick glance over my shoulder shows me my pursuer is not slowing down, so I race on, skidding across the floorboards as I try to remember which turns will lead me back to the foyer.

I can barely huff out a sigh of relief when I spot the front door, my lungs still seized with fear. Just as I'm about to collide with the splintering wood, Cornelius steps out of a room to my left.

"My, my, what's all this racket?" he asks, one curly, gray eyebrow raised high.

"Cornelius, what the hell? Why would you have one of your employees chase me out of the house when I'm trying to work?"

He looks almost offended. "Employees? My dear, I have no idea what you're talking about...I work alone."

"You what? But I–there was..." I sputter incoherently for a solid minute before I resort to just gesturing wordlessly to the corridor behind me.

"Oh ho ho, did someone have their first supernatural encounter?" He claps his motherfucking hands. "How exciting! It's been so many years since my own awakening, I've almost forgotten the thrill of it all."

I have to make a concerted effort to pick my jaw up off the floor. There's no way this wacky dude is trying to convince me I just saw my first ghost. *Absolutely not.* That thing was solid, creaking across floorboards and fucking around with light switches just to scare me.

"You might want to be a little more wary of who's coming and going in this place, Mr. Prescott. It seems your security is a little lax if any random idiot in a cloak can waltz in and start chasing people," I grumble to him as I try to smooth down my ruffled hair.

"A cloak?" He's unfazed by my suggestion. "How bizarre! None of the residents here are known to cavort in a cloak."

"Yeah, it's a total mystery." I roll my eyes, suddenly very irritated by the quirky character I found so amusing only half an hour ago. "I'll be seeing you, Mr. Prescott. I trust I'll be able to work undisturbed next time I visit."

With that, I wrench open the door and march back to my car, thoroughly sick of being the butt of yet another mean joke. One of these days I'll stop expecting anything to ever change around here.

10

DOMINIC

I GIVE the street a cursory glance before strolling up the short path to Shiloh's porch, conscious that there might be someone around who would take note of my visit. This is the first time I've dared to come here during daylight hours. Sneaking around at night simply isn't interesting enough anymore.

Or perhaps it doesn't bring me the same thrill it did the first time?

Either way, I can't fight the fierce compulsion to dig through every last corner of her home until I know it as well as my own.

I've been coming here every night since that first time after The Cauldron. Oftentimes, I choose a souvenir. Sometimes, I pick up a particularly dog-eared book, curious to know what story she was so drawn to that she'd read it a hundred times. Occasionally, I take a piece of clothing–something that smells like her. I always return them the next day, wondering if she's going mad searching for the moved or missing items.

Every night, it's the same routine. I move through the rooms methodically, picking apart her life piece by piece, and then I slip into her bedroom to watch her sleep...

Just for a few minutes.

Just to see her face settled in unconscious serenity, rather than screwed up in rage as it usually is when I'm near.

For the past two nights she's been locking her door, a mild inconvenience but nothing I can't handle quite easily. I deftly pick the lock, the tumblers clicking softly as I break through her meager defenses. The small victory is satisfying every time, as if I'm knocking straight through Shiloh's walls and rendering her completely vulnerable to me.

Today is no different. Although, now that she's at work for the day, I give myself the time to move slower through the little house. I could liken such freedom to having a woman tied up, completely at my mercy, while I do whatever I want with her. It's a potent kind of power, sauntering through Shiloh's home with all the relaxed ease of someone who owns the place. I can't help but smirk at the thought of how red she'd go with fury if she knew what I was doing. What I've *been* doing. Especially when I didn't bother to join her over the weekend for her visit to the Manor.

In truth, I just wasn't sure what I would do if I faced her so soon after our little *tiff*. After my own little meltdown at the B&B, I needed a breather. But I can't stay away for long. I never can, not now.

I move through the house with practiced stealth, familiarizing myself with how it all looks in the light. Every object, every cramped piece of furniture, holds a piece of her. I run my fingers along the spines of books on her shelves, imagining as I always do that she's done the same. That our hands are touching somehow just by brushing over the same surfaces.

I'm certain that soon this won't be enough. The craving to feel her skin against my own is becoming too much to bear. I don't know when my obsession truly became lustful...

Maybe it always was?

I wonder when the time comes how much she'll fight me at first, deny me her body until she finally realizes she wants this too–*or* will she surrender to me completely like a good little Shy Girl? I'm not entirely sure which I'd prefer.

My imagination drags me away from the present for a long while, until my cock is straining against my pants and I've lost focus on where I'm walking. But that's when I spot it. Just as I'm heading towards the kitchen–the door under the stairs is slightly ajar. I crouch slightly as I pull it open all the way, the squat cupboard far too low for my full height. The hinges creak loudly, making me freeze, until I remember that Shiloh isn't asleep upstairs this time. I have complete freedom to roam.

At first, the cupboard seems to hold nothing more than a slightly dusty collection of jackets and shoes, perhaps more suited for the summer months. But as I dig a little deeper, I find a crumpled box shoved way at the back. The dust is so much thicker here, clearly untouched for years. My pulse starts to race as I drag it out, curious as to the secrets I might find.

Lifting the lid, I try not to cough at the cloud of unsettled grime, blinking furiously until I can see more than an inch in front of my face again. What I find nearly stops my heart.

Her fucking pitiful poor-me journals.

Half a dozen leather-bound notebooks are tucked away in

the forgotten box. I grab the one on top with a feral hunger, fanning open the slightly yellowed pages until they land on a random entry.

> *October 15th, 2013*
>
> *Dom left today. Just packed up and waltzed off to New York with his dad, like it was nothing. Like we were nothing. Dad says he's not surprised, that he never wanted to be part of this family anyway. But the house feels so strange without him, too quiet.*
>
> *No more daily arguments, no more slamming doors. I thought I'd be happy with him gone. But I just feel more alone. How pathetic is that? He probably hasn't thought of me once.*
>
> *I hate him. I hate him so much it hurts. I hate him for leaving me. I hate him for making me miss him.*

My eyebrows pull closer together as I read. She'd barely looked at me the day I left, just mumbled a quiet *"whatever"* before disappearing into her room. I was sure she'd be happy to see the back of me. But apparently, we were both wrong– and her true feelings were just as shocking to her as they are to me now. I flip forward a few more pages, curiosity burning through me like a fever.

November 30th, 2013

I dreamed about him last night. I don't even want to write his name down anymore, I'm so sick of the sight of it.

We were running through the woods again. I pretended I hated it, as usual. But then he was on me, so close I could count his eyelashes. I wanted him to stay. Be still with me until I'd counted every last one.

What the hell is wrong with me? This is so messed up. I can never tell anyone. NEVER. I'll take this to my grave. I should burn this whole damn journal. Maybe even check myself into the psych ward for good measure.

He's my brother for heaven's sake!

I sit back on my heels, barely noticing the smears of dust marring my black slacks as my mind reels. Fifteen-year-old Shiloh had feelings... for *me*.

This is all just too delicious.

I can see the scene she paints dancing behind my eyelids, as if we're back there together. I can picture the rapid rise and fall of her chest as she pants beneath me; that blue flame sparking in her eyes as she glares up at me.

But it's not fury I see there in the scene anymore. The fire has turned molten. I see hunger. Lust. I see everything I missed.

I groan quietly to myself as my dick grows hard. If this gets much more torturous, blue balls just might be the death of me. I snap the journal shut, rifling through the box until I find the year that I first moved to Avalon. Ready for a trip down memory lane, I tuck the box back into its hiding place and retreat from the suffocating confines of the cupboard.

Shiloh's bed seems to beckon to me from the floor above. So, I decide to indulge myself, eager to be surrounded by her scent as I dive into her mind and relive those first few tumultuous months.

HOURS LATER, I'm *still* here, the sun long since set. And that's when I hear the telltale click of Shiloh's key turning in the front door.

Oh shit.

There's no chance I'll be able to slip out of her bedroom while she's right there at the bottom of the stairs. In a split-second decision, I dive under the bed, resigned to the fact that I'll have to wait until she takes a shower before I can sneak back out.

I clutch the journal to my chest as I hear her come up the stairs, careful to keep my breathing low and steady. Having her find me hiding beneath her bed is *not* how I'd like our next meeting to go. I silently curse myself for being so careless. This is so unlike me, I barely recognize myself in the moment. I'm always ten steps ahead, conducting my business with ruthless precision. Whatever insanity is fueling this obsession...

It's making me *sloppy.*

Shiloh's footsteps pause just inside the bedroom door. I hear the clanking of chains against porcelain as she presumably removes her jewelry and dumps it in one of those silly little dishes she has scattered all over the room. She sighs heavily, the springs in the mattress creaking loudly as she flops down onto the bed.

I'm acutely aware of how close she is. Just a few inches of wood and fabric separate us. I clench my fists, forcing down the fierce urge to crawl out and touch her. This was a mistake. I need to get out of here before I do something truly unforgivable.

But Shiloh doesn't move.

For a moment, I think she might have drifted off. I strain to hear her breathing, not taking the risk of moving until I'm certain she's fallen into some late-afternoon coma. But then a loud buzzing almost startles me out of my skin. From the sound of Shiloh's gasp, I figure she's just as shocked.

"Hey, Jem. What's up?" The mattress shifts as she hoists herself up the bed.

"No, I haven't heard from him. Haven't seen him either. Maybe he's gone." My lips curl in a satisfied smirk as I imagine her looking for me around town, perhaps glancing over her shoulder every so often in case I show up unexpectedly. I can't deny the thought amuses me, even if it's a game I haven't actually been playing.

"I don't know, Jem. Honestly, I have no idea. If he's skipped town, maybe Melanie will just harass him over the phone until he coughs up the funds he promised. I sure as fuck won't be bullied into chasing him…We'll just have to find another sponsor… I don't know, there must be somebody… Come on Jem, canceling isn't an option. I won't allow it. Hell, I'll wash every car in the state if it'll raise the money we need… We'll figure it out, okay? Try not to stress. I'll see you tomorrow. Bye."

Shiloh groans deeply this time, a harsh sound that tells me exactly how frustrated she is. I don't have to lay eyes on her to know she's got her lips pressed together in a thin line, her face pinched in a way that makes her look like she's about to explode. I can't wait to see how she'll react when she finds out I never left, and she's forced to be grateful I still have every intention of bankrolling her little party...

Well when I can bring myself to face her without immediately tearing her clothes off.

As if by some sick joke, my thoughts are dragged back to the present moment by the sound of a soft, breathy moan above me. My spine stiffens. The mattress creaks and shifts again. Another few seconds and there's no doubt in my mind exactly what is happening.

Shiloh moans again, the sound shooting straight through me like a drug. I bite my lip hard enough to taste blood as I fight against my own hungry groan. My dick is so hard in my pants, I think it might split the seams. I *almost* release a pained hiss.

But she's not stopping any time soon.

Fuck. Fuck. FUCK.

Soon enough, the urge is too strong to resist any longer. As Shiloh's lustful sounds grow louder, I take advantage of the cover to slowly unbuckle my belt and ease down my fly. It's a feat of pure willpower to stay silent as I begin to stroke myself in time to her rhythmic movements.

I can only imagine what she looks like right now – head thrown back into her pillow, luscious lips parted as she pants, her fingers working frantically between her spread thighs. The picture is almost enough to drive me wild, only the last fraying thread of my control keeping me from giving away my presence.

Shiloh's breath hitches, the creaking of the mattress springs growing more erratic as she works herself higher. I pump my fist furiously, my eyes rolling back in my head as a steady stream of precum makes my fingers slick. I imagine her tongue again, and almost feel it swirling around my crown before she sucks me deep.

"Oh fuck," she gasps above me, her breathy voice trembling as she no doubt rushes towards release. It's only too easy to convince myself that she's in my fantasy with me, panting a curse as we drive each other towards blissful oblivion.

With a shuddering cry, Shiloh's hips still. I picture her thighs clamping together as her orgasm rips through her, wave after wave. The sound of her climax is my undoing. I have to shove my fist into my mouth this time to muffle any sound as I spill hot cum all over my hand.

For a while, the only sound in the room is our breathing. I lie there, boneless and dazed, steadfastly ignoring the feeling of pathetic shame that gnaws at the edges of my consciousness.

What the fuck am I doing? Am I seriously losing control of myself?

I've never been a man who has to tiptoe around his desires. Never. I reach out and take what I want, unashamed. But this inability to control myself? *No.* It started out subtle, but now...

Fuck, I can't go on like this anymore.

The soft pad of Shiloh's feet startles me as she finally rolls off the bed and heads into the bathroom. I wait a few minutes while the shower runs before I shuffle out from underneath the bed.

Shoving my dick back into my slacks, I hastily buckle my belt as I make my way back down the stairs. The sorry state of my sticky boxers is a gross reminder of what I've been reduced to as I chase this renewed addiction.

Enough is enough.

I know Shiloh wanted me once, her diaries prove it. I'm not going to hold myself back from reigniting that curiosity in her. That hunger.

Consequences be damned, I want to hear those breathy moans again and again. I want to drag them out of her with my own hands.

And I won't rest until it's my name escaping those lips.

11

SHILOH

THE MOMENT I walk into my classroom on Tuesday morning, the fluorescent lights flicker to life. I try to ignore the creeping unease as I remind myself their erratic stuttering is due to the school's ancient electric wiring and nothing to do with some ghostly presence.

The incident at Fairchild Manor clings to me like a cobweb, refusing to be brushed aside no matter how many times I tell myself it was just a stupid prank. Not only that, but Dominic's infuriating disappearance after all his grand promises about funding the Ball nags at me day and night.

Pile all that in with the strange happenings at my house, and I'm just about ready to book myself in for a lobotomy.

I take a deep breath, inhaling the familiar scent of white-board markers and adolescent angst. It's calming, in its own way. I paste on what I hope is a convincing smile and walk to my desk, dropping my bag with a thud that echoes ominously in the empty room.

Get a fucking grip, Shiloh. It's just another day at work. Nothing creepy here.

Soon after, students begin to arrive in a cacophony of chatter and shuffling feet. I busy myself arranging my notes, pretending I don't notice the curious glances thrown my way. Do I look as disheveled as I feel? I smooth down my skirt, wishing I'd taken the time to iron it this morning instead of stumbling out the door like a mindless zombie.

I shove the regret aside and clear my throat. "Okay, everyone. Settle down. Books out, please. We're diving straight back into the Woman in Black this morning."

There's a collective groan from my sophomore class, punctuated by the rustle of backpacks and the flipping of book pages. My smile grows a little more genuine, the theatrical displays of displeasure a familiar comfort in this line of work.

"Alright, who can summarize the scene where Arthur Kipps sees the Woman in Black for the first time?" I ask, leaning against my desk as I settle into doing what I do best. "Anyone? Come on, guys, at least one of you must have done the reading. You're breaking my heart!"

I breathe a sigh of relief as a few hesitant hands are raised. I call on Amanda, a usually quiet girl in the back row who always has her nose buried in a book. No guesses for who she reminds me of.

"Um, so, Arthur is at Alice Drablow's funeral, and he notices this woman standing apart from everyone else. She looks all sick and like she's wasting away. Then, when he goes to approach her, she just like, vanishes."

"Excellent, Amanda, thank you. Now, what I want us to focus on today is how the author makes this scene particularly unsettling. What techniques does she use in the writing?"

The class sits silent yet again, a sea of blank faces staring back at me. I fight the urge to roll my eyes. It's going to be one of those days.

"Let's break it down, shall we? Start with the setting. Where is Arthur when this scene takes place?"

"In a church," someone calls out from the front row.

"Exactly," I say, turning to write it on the whiteboard. "And what is the weather like that day?"

"Foggy," another student pipes up. "Cold, I guess."

I nod encouragingly, adding the answers to my list. "A little bit of pathetic fallacy here, couldn't we say? What else makes this scene a little creepy?"

Slowly, but surely, more students find the courage to voice their thoughts. We talk through the use of sensory details, the way the author builds tensions through describing the main character's mounting unease. I'm sure I even see sparks of interest igniting in a few eyes, and it instantly improves my mood. This is why I became a teacher, to pass on my love of literature, to help my students see the magic that words can hold.

As the discussion picks up steam, I feel myself relaxing more than I have in a week. The events that have been plaguing me fade into the recesses of my mind, swept into the background while I'm engrossed in my chosen profession.

"I think the creepiest part," Jake, one of my more outspoken students, chimes in from his seat in the back row, "is how the Woman in Black just appears out of nowhere. Like, imagine you're just chilling at some stranger's funeral, and then *boom* there's this ghost lady lurking behind you. That would be freaky as hell."

A ripple of laughter spreads throughout the room at his apt assessment.

"I know I'd feel more than a little unsettled," I agree. "Hill does a great job of—"

"Kinda like that weirdo in the black robes who's been giving people heart attacks around Fairchild Manor," Jake cuts in, a mischievous grin curling his lips.

My lecture dies in my throat, the whiteboard marker almost slipping from my suddenly numb fingers. "Uh, sorry, what are you talking about?"

The class erupts in excited chatter, everyone talking over each other in response to my question. I struggle to make any sense of the jumble of voices, not least because my blood is pounding loudly in my ears.

"Sarah Meyers saw them last week."

"It's just some loser playing a weird prank."

"Nah, my mom thinks it might be a real ghost."

I throw my hands in the air, trying to regain some control of the room. "Hold up, hold up. One at a time, please. Jake, what's all this about?"

Jake leans back casually in his chair, clearly relishing being the center of attention. "Ah, it's just some prankster hanging around the Manor and the grounds. Freaking people out, you know? There's no way it's a real ghost, who the hell dresses like that? Unless it's the grim reaper." He tacks the last part on with a loud cackle, playing up to the class clown bravado.

I grip the edge of my desk where I lean against it, my knuckles turning white with the strain.

"Uh, you okay, Miss Wilson?" a soft voice from the front row spears through the hurricane blaring in my skull.

I blink a few times, realizing I must have been staring into space. The whole class is watching me, some looking concerned, others mockingly amused. I try to force a smile, though it undoubtedly reads more like a reluctant grimace. "I'm fine, thanks. Just...not especially pleased about all this. Does anyone know who's behind it?"

I wince as the discussion reignites in another frenzy, everyone chucking in their two cents about who they think it might be. It quickly becomes apparent that none of them actually have any idea who the culprit is.

"Okay, okay, that's enough of that," I call out, having to raise my voice louder than I would have liked. "While this is no doubt entertaining for all of you, we should get back to discussing literature. Or you're all going to fail the midterm."

Though the chatter dies down with another class-wide groan, I can still see a gleam of excitement in their eyes. They're all practically vibrating with the need to keep gossiping about Avalon's latest mystery.

"Before we continue," I say, adopting the no-nonsense teacher voice I don't often employ, "I should remind you all that trespassing is illegal. And harassing people, even if you're just playing a prank, can have serious consequences. Am I understood?"

I lock eyes with each of them in turn, praying that my warning dissuades anyone who might be involved. "I don't want to find out that any of you have been sneaking around Fairchild Manor, or anywhere else you shouldn't be, for that matter."

A chorus of mumbled confirmations echoes throughout the room. I give a satisfied nod and turn back to the board.

"Alright, let's take a look at some of the chapter's gothic elements..."

The rest of the lesson passes without further incident. I go through the motions on autopilot, teaching about foreshadowing and building atmosphere, but my mind is elsewhere. By the time the bell signals the end of the period, I'm almost stunned to find I'm still standing in the same spot.

I sink into my desk chair as the students scuttle out, still whispering excitedly about whoever this costumed phantom might be. Finally, I'm left completely alone with my thoughts. They swirl like fallen leaves caught in a gust of wind, chaotic and impossible to pin down.

It's a relief to know I didn't imagine the cloaked figure chasing me through the house on Saturday. But the revelation only brings with it a host of accompanying questions. Who could it be? Will they be caught soon? Do they have anything to do with all the weird stuff going on at my house?

The thought causes me to squirm nervously in my seat. If a student has been breaking into my home, that's a whole other level of inappropriate. I may have to do more than just locking my door... Maybe self-defense classes? *Something.*

I'm startled out of my musing by a sudden loud buzz. I fish my phone out of my bag, my already-exhausted heart kicking up a gear when I see Dominic's name appear on the screen. In all the chaos of discussing this mystery figure, I'd almost forgotten he existed. *Almost.*

The text is brief with no invitation for debate.

> DOMINIC: WE NEED TO GET DOWN TO
> PLANNING THIS COSTUME PARTY. I'LL COME
> BY YOUR PLACE AFTER SCHOOL IS OUT.

I stare at the message, unsure whether to be relieved or

irritated. It's clear he doesn't intend to abandon us as the sponsor, but who the hell does he think he is dictating to me when and where we'll meet? Inviting himself into my home, of all places.

My thumbs fly over the screen as I type and delete several increasingly furious responses before I settle with just *liking* the text. I tell myself I should be pleased he hasn't disappeared into the ether and taken his money with him. But, of course, I can't entirely quash the nagging rage that turns my vision red every time I'm reminded of how he's crashed through my simple life like a damn bulldozer.

And then there's this other nagging feeling.

A quiet thrill that comes completely out of left field. There's a part of me that wants to keep my estranged stepbrother close, holding him to me as if we might get a second chance to fix whatever is broken between us and actually mean something to each other.

"You've been alone too fucking long, Shiloh," I mutter to myself, pinching the bridge of my nose between my thumb and finger. "He doesn't want to be part of your screwed up family."

I feel like I'm trapped in a haunted house all of my own, one where the ghosts hail from a past I'd rather forget, and the monster dressed in black is only too real. The rest of the school day passes in a blur of grading papers and lecturing to uninterested teenagers, my mind constantly drifting back to Dominic's text and the looming specter of our meeting.

12

DOMINIC

IT'S A SLIGHTLY JARRING FEELING WALKING up to Shiloh's house knowing this time I'm actually supposed to be here, and that she'll be fully aware of my presence. But even with that, I hesitate only half a second before rapping my knuckles against the chipped paint of her front door.

I mean, now that I've spent some time thinking about it, I've made up my mind. I don't want to sneak around anymore. My craving has...*evolved.*

I want to be able to look at her, breathe her in, invade her space. After reading her journal, I'm more convinced than ever she won't push me away. Maybe at first she'll try, but then I know she'll give in. She has the same craving I do.

And I'll do whatever it takes to get it out of her.

The door swings open abruptly, revealing an already-disgruntled Shiloh. Her blonde waves are piled messily atop her head, stray tendrils framing a face etched with irritation. I take in the short black skirt, paired with an oversized T-shirt. She has no idea how hard she's making this for me.

"Where the hell were you on Saturday?" she immediately demands, wasting no time it seems.

"Hello to you too, Shy Girl," I drawl, stepping inside without an invitation. Her scowl deepens at the nickname, though it slipped from my lips without a second thought. Clearly, I'm going to have to be a little more appeasing if we're going to get through this without her trying to stab me.

"I had some urgent business to take care of. Besides, it didn't sound like a task you'd struggle to get through alone."

The words come out slightly more mocking than I'd intended, but they have the desired effect of halting her interrogation. A twinge of regret tugs at my gut seeing her face fall slightly. The Shiloh I once knew hated to be thought of as incapable.

"Let's get this moving, shall we?" I say, making my way through to the living room. I shrug off my overcoat and drape it over the back of the couch, noting once again that Shiloh's attention appears fixed on my gloves–just like at the coffee house. She stares at them, a little crease forming between her brows, as if they unnerve her in some way.

That will be fun to play with.

"Tell me about whatever plans you have so far. Décor ideas? Themed cocktails? I assume you've thought of something more compelling than just 'spooky' and 'orange'."

She rolls her eyes, snapping out of whatever trance she was in while staring at the gloves I'm now peeling off. "I'm not entirely sure where I'm going with it yet," she mumbles, gesturing vaguely towards the papers spread across the coffee table. "I've been researching local legends, looking for something we might be able to incorporate into the masquerade theme. Melanie shot down my idea to celebrate Avalon's history and lore, but I might be able to weave some of it into her stupid theme anyway."

"Not bad," I admit, picking up a rough sketch of what looks like masked figures dancing around a bonfire, "though I think pyrotechnics might be off the table."

Shiloh's shoulders visibly relax as she huffs a low chuckle, snatching the paper out of my hand. I settle myself into the nearest armchair, waiting until she sinks into the couch to continue our discussion. It doesn't escape my notice that she chooses the end furthest away from me.

"You look like you haven't slept in days," I murmur, the words falling from my lips before I can stop them. I hadn't intended to make the observation out loud, but my attention was held hostage by the dark circles marring the pale skin under her eyes.

Shiloh scoffs, shooting me a look that tells me she didn't find my comment particularly flattering. "I've had a lot on my mind lately." I find myself holding my breath as she runs her hand through her disheveled hair.

Focus.

I clear my throat. "Please don't tell me, you've run out of ideas to get teenagers interested in Shakespeare."

She barely reacts, her expression unmoving. "You're hilarious."

"I try." I can't contain the smirk that lifts one corner of my mouth, this rare moment of levity being something I could get used to. "Seriously, what's eating you? You seem...on edge. More than usual, I mean."

I watch her carefully, half-expecting this to be the moment she accuses me of breaking in. But the next words out of her mouth catch me completely off guard.

"I think..." she starts and then trails off, chewing on her lower lip in a way that has me hungry to feel it between my own teeth. "I think one of my students might be stalking me."

For a second, I'm certain I misheard. "The fuck are you talking about?"

Shiloh shifts uncomfortably in her seat, pointedly avoiding my gaze. "I know, I know. It sounds crazy, but weird things have been happening. I keep finding my stuff in places I didn't leave them in and had to start locking my door at night. Then the other day at Fairchild Manor, during the tour you so graciously left me to do alone, someone chased me out of the house. My students think there's some prankster dressing up in a black cloak and scaring people. Maybe the culprit is breaking into other houses too... I don't know."

She drops her head into her hands and rubs at her eyes, as if she might dispel the anxiety like a bad dream. I don't respond immediately, silently outraged that some other faceless threat is occupying her thoughts. I don't like to share.

"I'm sure it's nothing," I eventually say, waving my hand dismissively. "You know what teenagers are like, they do dumb shit. I doubt any of them would be brave enough to actually break into your house, though."

"You're probably right," she sighs. "Maybe the stress of this whole Halloween Ball business is getting to me. I know you don't care and this is just some joke to you..." Shiloh pauses, sighing. "But I really don't want to screw it up."

I struggle not to roll my eyes at her, determined to avoid another verbal knife fight. "Well, now that my name's on it, it has to go well. I refuse to let you embarrass me, so these ideas of yours had better pan out."

To my surprise, she chuckles again, a nervous titter that

doesn't quite reach her eyes. "So glad to have you on side, Dom," she says wryly. Something in my chest clenches at the nickname. No one has called me Dom in eleven years. At least, any time some random hookup has made that attempt at familiarity I've shut it down.

"Any time, Shy. Now, how about you be a gracious hostess and offer me a drink? Party planning is thirsty work." I make sure to infuse enough humor in my tone so that she doesn't immediately lose her temper. It seems to work.

"Sure, I guess. Is Merlot okay? I'm pretty sure that's all I have."

I nod once and she ambles off to the kitchen. Her hands are shaking slightly when she comes back in with two overly full glasses, the dark liquid sloshing perilously close to the rim.

"The fuck, Shiloh. Do you have a drinking problem I should be aware of?"

"What? N-no!" she stutters, dumping my drink onto the coffee table in front of me instead of putting it straight into my hand. "I've just had a stressful week, okay?"

"It's Tuesday," I deadpan.

This time she really laughs, a bubbly, melodic sound that's more intoxicating than any alcohol. My eyebrows shoot up almost into my hairline when she plops herself back down onto the couch, this time at the end nearest me. I try not to focus too hard on the scant inches left between our knees.

"You know..." She takes a deep breath, and then meets my gaze head on. "Do you really have to torture me all the time? How long are you sticking around for anyway? In town, I mean." I can tell she's trying hard to keep her tone casual, but there's an obvious anxiety in the tightness around her eyes and the set of her shoulders.

The urge to see her submit to me hits me in a fresh wave of heat. I want to see her defeated, succumbing to her own desire to have me near. I know she hasn't forgotten.

"Always so eager to get rid of me, damn," I taunt her. "Anyone could think it was *you* trying to torture *me*."

She scoffs again. "Actually, I was just thinking that it's kinda nice to no longer be the lone wolf of the family. With you here, dad and Viv might remember that I'm the one they prefer having around."

I can't help but raise an eyebrow at her strange choice of words. "I wouldn't call *you* a lone wolf. More like a black sheep." *Innocent. Helpless. Sometimes pathetic.*

"Whatever." She knocks her fist against my shoulder, the unexpected contact leaving goosebumps beneath my shirt. "I just meant, it's nice to feel like I'm not the only outsider in this weird, disconnected family we're both part of."

Her confession hits me straight in the gut, stirring up that guilt I would much rather keep buried. I take a long sip of wine. It's not pleasant, and is definitely cheap, but it's a welcome opportunity to compose a response.

"What do you mean?" I press, curiosity getting the better of me.

She goes back to avoiding eye contact, swirling her wine in her glass as she stares into it like some magic mirror that holds all the answers. "It's just... I moved back here after college so that I could stay close to them all, to try and be a big sister to the little ones. Yet, it feels like each year they all drift further away. Like I'm not...not needed. You're lucky your dad wants you by his side at the company, Viv and mine couldn't care less about me. I live close, but they don't check on me for *weeks*."

Now it's my turn to scoff. "Trust me Shy, there's nothing lucky about being close to my father." The bitterness in my tone obviously surprises her, though it's a taste I've long been familiar with.

"What was it like?" she asks softly. If I'm not mistaken, genuine concern shines in those icy blue eyes. "We never heard from you after you left. I just assumed you were having the time of your life, happy to be rid of this place."

"I was nothing but a necessity to him–his sole heir. He wanted me to be successful, but if I was, it threatened his ego. Every accomplishment was met with criticism instead of praise. I was just another 'failed investment,' as he liked to put it." *Never mind the brass knuckles he used as* enforcement. She doesn't need to know about that.

Shiloh winces. "That sounds awful. I'm sorry you had to grow up that way."

I shrug, not entirely unhappy with the weirdly vulnerable direction this conversation has taken. "It made me who I am today. And when I take over the company, I'll propel us all forward beyond even his wildest dreams. I hope the sudden realization of his own inferiority gives him a heart attack."

"I believe it," she chuckles. "If anyone can do it, you can."

"If I'm not mistaken, that almost sounded like a compliment."

"I guess it was." Shiloh frowns, as if she's just as stunned by the revelation as I am. "I just, um..." She leans forward slightly, her glass clenched in both hands. "I'm tired of the fighting, Dom. We're not kids anymore. We could be...*friends*, maybe. Don't you want that?"

She lends weight to the question by reaching out a hand and laying it on my knee. The touch is light, barely there, but it sends a jolt through me like I've been struck by lightning. I look down at that hand, then up at her face. Her eyes are wide, staring down at where she's made contact as if she can't quite believe she's the master of her own body.

"Shiloh," I murmur, placing my fingers under her chin and pushing it up until she looks at me. The quiet gasp she lets slip is my undoing. Before I can think better of it, I close the distance between us and capture her plump lips with mine.

13

SHILOH

FOR MAYBE A FEW SECONDS, I'm lost in the daring brush of Dom's lips, the scrape of his stubble over my skin.

Then, all at once the truth of what's happening crashes into me with the force of a semi truck. I shove against his chest with a yelp, leaping up from the couch and stumbling back several paces.

"What the fuck are you doing?" I demand, my voice shaking far more than I'd like.

Dom's eyes seem to glint dangerously as he leans back, sprawling in the armchair like it's his throne. His lips curl up in that mocking smirk that somehow makes *me* feel ashamed.

"Come on, Shy Girl. We both know you wanted that as much as I did," he drawls, his voice taking on a husky tone that tells me exactly where his mind is at. "It was written all over your face."

I shake my head violently enough to bruise my own brain, desperately willing away the flush I can feel creeping up my neck.

"That's insane! I wasn't–I don't...You're my *brother*, for fuck's sake!"

A low chuckle rumbles from Dom's chest as he slowly stands, like a predator unfurling its muscles before it launches into an attack. "Stepbrother," he corrects, taking a deliberate step in my direction. "And barely that. Don't lie to me, Shiloh, I'd bet good money those pretty panties of yours are drenched right now."

"You're sick," I spit, but even to my own ears, the words lack conviction. My face is burning hotter with each passing second, betraying me. I take another hesitant step back, until I feel my spine hit the wall. *Trapped.*

Dom's dark eyes rake over me like he has all the time in the world to devour his prey. It's like he's removing each piece of my clothing one by one, without even lifting a finger. I squeeze my thighs together, desperately trying to ignore the traitorous heat that's pooling between them.

"You will never touch me," I seethe, summoning every ounce of venom I can muster. "We're siblings. This is so wrong. On every level!"

His answering grin is pure black magic. "Have it your way."

His gaze never leaves mine as he reaches over to where he draped his coat on the back of the couch. I watch in horror as he pulls on each of his leather gloves, the soft creaking of the buttery fabric almost deafening in the silence between us.

"I don't have to touch you to make you scream."

He advances on me again. I should run. I should scream. I should do anything other than stand here, pinned by his heated stare like a butterfly on a corkboard. But my muscles won't listen to me, my voice locked away in some safe I can't crack open.

This is Dom, my stepbrother. The same insufferable monster who used to taunt me mercilessly, and made my life a living hell any chance he got. So why does my body thrum at the promise of him claiming me? Why does some treacherous part of my soul hunger for him to pin me down like he did so many times when we were younger?

As if the last eleven years never happened, I'm right back to drowning in confusion. Desire warring with disgust in a violent battle where nobody wins. Dom towers over me now, close enough that I can feel his breath warm my already burning skin.

He raises one gloved hand slowly, as if trying not to spook me, and grasps my jaw between his fingers and thumb.

"Stop fighting yourself, Shy Girl. You don't want to fight anymore, remember? Kiss me," Dom commands.

At some point, between the closeness of his lips and the strong grip he has on my face, I stop thinking altogether. My body seems to move of its own volition, my hands fisting in his shirt and wrenching him towards me.

His deep groan tangles with my helpless whimper as our lips meet for the second time. He wastes no time plunging his tongue in my mouth, asserting his dominance in a way that's so utterly him. But rather than fight against it like I tried to do for so many years, I let it overpower me. My knees start to shake until it's possible only his hold on my jaw is keeping me upright.

He tastes like red wine and forbidden fruit, and I drink him in greedily over and over again.

Dom's other hand slides up to cup my breast over my

shirt. Even through layers of fabric, the heat of his touch brands me in a way I'm not sure I'll ever be able to erase. I immediately arch into his palm, shamelessly desperate for more.

How long has it been since a man touched me like this? Since I felt this wanted, this fiercely desired? In this moment I can't recall ever being touched at all. Dom kneads my flesh roughly, until I'm squirming and panting in his gloved hands.

I should be disgusted. I should push him away again. But God help me, I can't bring myself to end this.

My own hands are still fisted in Dom's shirt, trapped between our bodies where I can feel the press of his solid chest. Clearly hungry for us to be closer still, he shoves his thigh between my legs, and I don't even have to command the movement before I'm wantonly grinding against it, chasing some friction to soothe the fire blazing in my underwear.

Dom's lips finally leave mine, he trails them along my jaw before grazing his teeth down my earlobe.

"That's it, Shy Girl," he growls. "Show me how bad you want this. You *need* it."

All I can do is whimper again while he nips at my neck, his deft fingers somehow finding my puckered nipples, still confined within the fabric of my bra.

"Dom," I pant, struggling to form any sort of coherent thought. "We shouldn't…"

But even as the half-hearted protest leaves my lips, my hips continue to rock against him. Dom's dark chuckle hums against the sensitive skin below my ear. "Your body disagrees," he murmurs there.

He suddenly withdraws both his hands, only to reach out again to catch me as I almost crumple to the floor at his feet.

His grip on my waist is strong, possessive almost, as his fingers sink into the soft flesh at my waist. I almost lose my balance again as he spins me, pulling me away from where he had me caged against the wall.

"Turn around."

I blink up at him, in such a daze I can't quite compute the order. Dom's eyes narrow almost imperceptibly, but the effect is terrifying all the same.

"Now, Shiloh."

My body obeys before my mind can catch up. Dom's solid warmth is now pressed against my back, his hands reclaiming their possessive grip on my hips.

"Bend over," he orders, another husky rumble in my ear. "Hold on to the back of the couch."

I don't know who I've become in the last few minutes, but I comply without hesitation, my fingers gripping the threadbare fabric of my second-hand sofa. Dom's leatherbound fingers skate up the backs of my thighs, hoisting my skirt up to my hips and leaving goosebumps in their wake.

I squeeze my eyes shut, grateful for the small mercy that I don't have to look at him while he touches me in all the ways he shouldn't. If I can't see his face, maybe I can pretend it isn't him, and this is just a vivid fantasy I've conjured after too many hours alone. This isn't my stepbrother about to... to...

The thought trails off completely as Dom hooks his fingers into my underwear, dragging the fabric down at a torturously slow pace. I bite my lips to stifle an ungodly moan as the cool leather of his gloves slides against my exposed flesh. I had no idea fucking *gloves* would be such a turn on.

"Look at you," Dom almost purrs, his hands coming back up to roughly squeeze my ass, pulling the cheeks apart. "So wet for me. I should have placed that bet after all. But still, I intend to cash in."

I don't respond, can't respond. My whole universe has narrowed to the points where Dom is touching me, to the ache that's grown to an almost painful roar between my thighs. I arch my back, silently begging him not to stop.

A single gloved finger traces a path straight down my slit, gliding through the slickness there. If I were thinking straight right now, I might marvel at how turned on I am, and that it's my own stepbrother who's reduced me to a mere puddle.

But I'm not thinking at all. Even less so when he plunges two fingers inside me without warning. I cry out, my pussy instinctively clenching against the intrusion. It's been so long, the stretch burns in the most addictive way. Dom sets a punishing pace, curling his fingers to hit that spot that has my eyes rolling back in my head.

I wouldn't be surprised to find myself drooling over the couch cushions. I'm lost to sensation, reduced to a panting, moaning wreck as he fucks me with his fingers. The leather adds a delicious friction I hadn't ever imagined in my fantasies.

Just please don't stop.

I barely notice when I start rocking my hips, meeting each thrust of his fingers with pure lusty greed.

"That's it. Take what you need," Dom praises me. "Show me how much you love my fingers in this sweet little cunt." His crude commands should shock me, and snap me out of this desperate haze.

Instead, they only stoke the raging inferno burning in my core. I'm so close, teetering on the precipice. Just a little more...

I let out a strangled whimper when Dom suddenly withdraws his fingers. It chokes off completely when I hear the telltale sound of a zipper being dragged down. I catch my breath, and brace.

I don't need to see what's happening to know that it's the head of Dom's cock that I feel brushing through my dripping pussy, hot and insistent. A weak voice in the back of my mind screams at me that this is the point of no return, but it's drowned out by the pounding of blood in my ears and the throbbing need between my legs.

Of course, Dom doesn't ask for permission. He shoves himself inside me with one powerful thrust, stretching me to my limits. I yelp, the heady mix of pain and pleasure quickly turning it into a feral groan. He doesn't give me time to adjust to his substantial fucking size, immediately setting a brutal pace that has my couch creaking beneath me.

"Fuck, Shiloh," Dom grunts, his hips–still clad in the slacks he hasn't bothered to remove–snapping against my ass. "You're so fucking tight. Even better than I imagined."

His words stir something in me, a fresh wave of heat licking up my spine.

He's imagined this? Fantasized about how it might feel to be inside me?

The thought is intoxicating. I find myself pushing back to meet him again, thrust for thrust, chasing the impossible fullness like it's the last time I'll ever be fucked.

"Good girl," he groans. "Take it all."

Dom's cock hits places inside of me I didn't even know existed. It's so wrong, but now that he's there, I *don't* want it to stop.

When he snakes a gloved hand around my hip, expert

fingers seeking out my clit, and I see stars. The first brush of leather against the throbbing bundle of nerves has me almost sobbing into the crook of my elbow, my arms long since given up on keeping me upright.

"You gonna come for me, Shy Girl?" Dom's voice is getting strained, his rhythm faltering slightly as I'm sure he's sprinting towards his own release. "Is your little cunt gonna come all over your big brother's cock?"

His filthy words push me straight over the cliff. My orgasm barrels through me like a freight train, my vision whiting out as my body convulses over and over.

With a guttural groan Dom follows right after, my clenching pussy milking him for all he's worth. I moan breathlessly as he fills me, his own heavy breaths ringing in my ears as his relentless pounding finally slows.

I get maybe five glorious seconds of post-orgasmic haze before the harsh wave of reality crashes over me. I'm overcome with a revulsion so noxious it nearly leaves me gagging.

"Get off!" I shriek, shoving myself upright with a desperation to get him out of me. "Get *out.* Get out of my house, and leave me alone!"

I shove back against him and whirl around, almost tipping myself straight over the back of the couch in the process. Yanking my skirt back down, I feel the warm trickle of his cum seep down my thigh. The urge to retch only intensifies.

Dom's expression remains infuriatingly smug as he tucks himself back into his slacks. "Come on, Shiloh," he drawls. "You already trying to convince yourself you didn't love every fucking second of what we just did?"

"*Out*," I scream, grabbing the nearest book and hurling it at his head. "Don't ever fucking come back!"

His smirk morphs into a deep scowl as he smoothly dodges the book flying right at his face. But without argument, he grabs his coat and storms straight for the door. He slams it behind himself so forcefully I worry the entire frame will crumble into splinters.

The second he's gone, I bolt upstairs and throw myself straight into the bathroom, tearing off my clothes as I go. I need to be rid of his fucking scent. I turn the shower on full blast, not even waiting for the water to heat up before stepping under the spray. The stab of icy needles against my skin is a welcome punishment for what I just let happen.

I furiously scrub at my skin, as if I can wash away the memory of Dom's touch along with the physical evidence he left behind. Soap suds swirl down the drain, but I still feel every bit as filthy as when I started.

How could I let things go so far? What the fuck came over me?

I have a newfound understanding of the term 'temporary insanity', and I'll plead that case until I'm blue in the face.

It has to be stress, I tell myself. All this pressure trying to plan the Ball with Melanie breathing down my neck, this possible stalker situation that's had me tossing and turning at night–it's all just getting to me.

That's the only possible explanation. There's no way I would have let Dom touch me if I were in my right mind.

But even as I try to rationalize such a twisted turn of events, I know every bit of it is a lie. Truth is, I've wanted Dom to overpower me like that since the first time he ever commanded me to run from him, like I'm nothing more than his plaything. And now that it's happened, I'm terrified by how good it felt.

I stay in the shower long after the hot water runs out, praying the violent shivering will shake some sense into me.

It was all just a dark fantasy when we were teenagers. Nothing more than a sick craving I only confessed to the pages of my diary. It was never supposed to come true.

I'm an adult now. I'm supposed to have better self-control. I'm supposed to pay my fucking taxes and not fuck my fucking stepbrother.

When I finally step out of the shower, I catch sight of myself in the foggy mirror and grimace. Sodden hair plastered to my skull, eyes wide and haunted, I barely recognize the woman staring back at me.

"It was a mistake," I mutter to myself. "It won't happen again." Even if *he* is a deranged psychopath, *I* don't have to be a part of his twisted games.

I only wish I could believe it.

14

DOMINIC

I STRIDE out of Shiloh's little house like a wild animal on a rampage, my jaw clenched tight enough to break bone. My cock is still half-hard, straining against my zipper like it's trying to drag me back inside.

Fuck.

I've never been thrown out of a woman's home before. Especially not after fucking her brains out. The bitter taste of it clashes with the lingering flavor of Shiloh still on my tongue. I want to march right back in there and show her exactly who she's rejecting. I want to bend her over that ratty couch and fuck her again and again, until she can't remember her own name, let alone why she thought pushing me away was the right call.

But I don't. Because apparently, I'm a goddamn gentleman now.

The walk back to my B&B passes in an uncomfortable storm of frustration and arousal. I barely notice where I'm headed, trusting my feet to remember the route while my mind is a million miles away. A few locals are still out and about, calling cheerful greetings that I pointedly ignore. Let them think I'm the asshole from the big city who can't be bothered with small town pleasantries. It's the truth.

When I finally make it back, I slam the door of my room behind me, already yanking at my tie. The rest of my rumpled clothes hit the floor in a haphazard trail as I make my way into the bathroom. I step straight into the shower, hissing as the too-hot water hits my skin.

Closing my eyes, I'm immediately assaulted by vivid images of Shiloh. The way her lips parted on a gasp when I backed her against that wall. The curve of her back as she arched into my touch. The breathy little sounds she made when I entered her tight little cunt...

My hand drifts lower of its own accord, wrapping around my cock. I'm fully hard again, aching with the need to relive every second of what we just did. It would be so easy to jerk off right here, replaying the scene until my balls are completely empty.

But I'm too angry. Too conflicted about the uneasy feeling that settled like lead in my gut when Shiloh forced me out of her house.

With a snarl of frustration, I wrench my hand away. I scrub myself clean with harsh, efficient movements, refusing to linger on any part of my body that still longs for her touch.

I dry off quickly, the scrape of the cheap towel souring my dark mood even further. After pulling on a pair of clean boxers, I retrieve Shiloh's journal from its pride of place on my nightstand. Soon, I'll have to slip back into her house and switch it out for the next one, having made it through most of this year's scribblings. Settling into the creaky bed, I flip it open to the latest entries that I haven't yet studied.

September 5th, 2009
Dom called me shy girl outside school today, and now the nickname is spreading through my class. Why would he do that to me? I don't know what I did to make him hate me so much. I wish Vivienne had never brought him here.

The words hit me like a punch to the gut. I'd forgotten how much of a little shit I was back then, to an eleven-year-old girl who didn't deserve it. Shiloh's messy handwriting continues, detailing every slight and prank with painful clarity.

September 15th, 2009
Dom put a carving knife in my backpack today. I screamed when I opened it in class, and everyone laughed. Miss Johnson made me stand out in the hall until I calmed down. I cried the whole time. Dom acted like he had nothing to do with it when I got home and told Dad. I don't understand why he has to be so scary. I could have really hurt myself on that thing.

I let my head drop back against the wall, suddenly reluctant to read any more. The guilt stirring in my chest is an unfamiliar sensation. I'm not used to caring about the consequences of my actions, especially not ones from over a decade ago. But seeing it all laid out in Shiloh's childish scrawl... *fuck.*

Maybe I was too hard on her.

Another cruel incident flashes through my mind. Shiloh, soaking wet and near tears after I'd pushed her into the creek by our house just when we were heading to school. I'd laughed so hard then, reveling in my power over her. In how much weaker she was than me. Now, the memory just makes me feel sick.

I toss the diary aside, scrubbing a hand over my face. This isn't me. I don't do guilt or regret or any of that touchy-feely bullshit. I'm Dominic fucking Blackwood. I take what I want, and I don't apologize for it.

But Shiloh...

She's always been different. Even back then, when I was doing my damnedest to make her life hell, there was something about her that got under my skin. Something that made me want to push harder, to see how far I could go before she broke completely.

And now? That sick obsession is back with a vengeance. I want to shatter her apart with pleasure *and* pain. I want to hear my name on her lips as she comes undone beneath me, just like she did bent over that couch.

I groan, pressing the heels of my hands against my eyes. It seems incredibly unlikely I'll get the chance, after the way she freaked out while my cock was still buried inside her. But as I lie there in the darkness, all I can think about is the taste of her lips and the soft curves of her body pressed against mine. And I know I'll do whatever I can to bring her around.

The shrill ring of my phone cuts through the silence, startling me out of my Shiloh-induced daze. I glance at the screen, my father's name flashing like a damn nuclear missile warning. For a moment, I consider ignoring it. But that would only delay the inevitable.

"What?" I bark into the mic.

"Dominic." My father's voice is sharp, all business. "Get back to New York. *Now.*"

I scoff, settling back against the pillows for what will no doubt be a jolly little chat. "I'm on vacation, old man. Remember?"

"Vacation's over. We're pushing through the Hartley deal, and I need your...particular expertise."

"I made sure they understood the consequences of getting too ambitious in their negotiations," I remind him, flexing my fist at the memory. The satisfying crunch of bone beneath my knuckles and the way that pompous prick had whimpered and begged come flooding back to mind. "What more do you want from me?"

"I want you to do your job," he snaps. "Or have you forgotten your responsibilities while you've been off playing tourist?"

I roll my eyes, though I know he can't see it. "I haven't forgotten anything. But I'm not done here yet. I've more than earned this break and you fucking know it."

"Done with what, exactly? What could possibly be more important than the future of this company?"

The image of Shiloh, flushed and writhing beneath me, flashes through my mind unbidden.

"That's none of your business," I answer curtly, forcing my brain to stay on track. "I'll be back when I'm good and ready. The Hartley deal will go through just fine without any more input from me."

"Dammit, Dominic!" Dante Blackwood's infamous composure finally cracks. "Do you have any idea how much work I've put into this? How many years I've spent planning this takeover? And you're disappearing at the last hurdle for what? Some backwater fling? Have you been pussy whipped by a fucking skunk? Or is it drugs? Whatever you're shoving up your nose, save it until the deal of the decade is fucking sealed."

I bristle at his harsh accusations, anger coiling hot in my gut. "Watch your mouth, Dante. You might be my father, but don't forget who really keeps this company afloat. Also," I spat, "I really don't think you can talk much about snorting illegal substances."

"Is that a threat?" He laughs, but there's no humor in it, just biting disdain. "You ungrateful little shit. After everything I've done for you–"

I hang up the phone.

For a moment, I consider hurling it across the room. But that would mean he'd gotten to me. So instead, I set it on my nightstand with exaggerated care, my movements slow and deliberate as I try to rein in my overboiling temper.

I don't need his shit. I've spent my entire life trying to live up to his impossible standards, and for what? To be called a disappointment? To be reminded, yet again, that I'll never be good enough in his eyes?

Fuck that. Fuck him. If the deal tanks, he'll finally have to admit that I'm the one in charge. Blackwood Enterprises would fall apart without me. Hell, maybe it already is. I'm struggling to find a fuck to give.

My gaze lands on Shiloh's journal, still lying open on the bed beside me, a glaring reminder of the miserable little demon my father bred me to be. I find myself picking it up again, flipping through the pages until I find the entry for a particular date I'm curious to read her thoughts on.

> *December 25th, 2009*
> *I can't believe it. Dom actually got me a Christmas present! It's just a mood ring from the dollar store, but still. He even tried to pretend it was from Santa, but I saw him sneak it under the tree last night. Maybe he's not so bad after all.*

I can't help but chuckle to myself at little Shiloh's stunned excitement. I remember that ring. I'd stolen it, actually, from a girl in my class who'd been stupid enough to leave it on her desk during chem lab. But I'd given it to Shiloh because... *why?*

Maybe because I'd seen how sad she looked when she thought no one was paying attention? Maybe because even then, some part of me had wanted to make her smile? Even when I was usually the one making her cry in the first place.

She was a toy to me. A puppet I knew how to make dance. I was more of a chip off the old Blackwood block than I realized.

The memory of her face lighting up when she'd opened that cheap little trinket sends an odd warmth spreading through my veins. It's quickly doused by a wave of shame when I recall how I'd ruined the moment by telling her that Santa was an old creep who probably touched little kids.

I'd been so determined to push her away, to prove that I didn't care. That I didn't need anyone. But maybe...

Maybe I'd just been as screwed up and miserable as she was.

God knows our parents didn't care enough to do anything about it.

The realization is uncomfortable, to say the least. I'm not used to questioning myself like this. I'm not used to feeling...anything, really. Beyond anger and lust and the cold satisfaction of getting what I want.

But Shiloh makes me feel things I can't even name–things I'm not sure I want to examine too closely.

I banish the thought, focusing instead on reliving the twisted victory I achieved today. The softness of her flesh in my hands. The way her body fit against mine, like we were two pieces of the same broken puzzle. The taste of her blushed lips after she'd nervously gulped that shitty wine.

Fuck, her lips. I close my eyes again, losing myself in the memory of our kiss. The second one. The one she let herself actually enjoy. I remember the tentative press of her mouth against mine that quickly gave way to heated passion. The little gasp she'd let slip when I'd dragged my teeth down her earlobe. The way her fingers had fisted in my shirt, pulling me closer like she couldn't get enough of me.

I want more. I want to explore every inch of her body with my hands, my mouth. I want to hear her cry out my name as I bury myself inside her. I want...

I want *her*. All of her. In a way I've never wanted anyone before.

15

SHILOH

I SHOWED up at school way too early this morning, just in my desperation to be out of the house. I can't help feeling like Dom has left his rotting mark on the place, like the scent of what we did last night still festers in my living room. I'll have to spray Lysol on every cushion within an inch of its life just to feel like I can't smell him anymore.

As I enter my classroom, the familiar surroundings calm my nerves. This is my domain. My fingers trail along the graffitied table tops as I make my way to my own desk. Various lesson plans scattered across its surface demand my attention, but I have no doubt that focusing on anything other than the memory of Dom's gloved hands on my skin will be a Herculean effort today.

I grab a red pen and start marking pop quizzes with more force than necessary. The scratching sound fills the quiet room as I lose myself in the task, undoubtedly scoring a little more harshly than I would on a day when my mood was a little brighter. Just as I'm starting to feel somewhat normal again, a knock at the door disturbs my peace.

"Come in," I call, confused as to why a student or another teacher would knock instead of walking straight in. First period starts soon, I can already hear most of the student body chattering in the halls.

To my surprise, Lloyd from the post office steps in, arms full of an enormous flower arrangement. The bouquet overflows with bright red and fuchsia blooms, in varieties I can't name. My jaw drops as he places it on my desk, obscuring half my workspace in the process.

"Delivery for Miss Shiloh Wilson," he announces gleefully, holding out a clipboard. "Sign here, please."

I scribble my signature absentmindedly, acutely aware of the whispers and giggles erupting from the students who've begun filtering into the classroom. Heat creeps up my neck as I bid Lloyd farewell with a mumbled thanks.

"Ooh, Miss Wilson! Who are those from?" Liz, the most notoriously popular–and very mean–girl from the junior class squeals as she saunters through the door.

"That's none of your business," I reply evenly, trying my best to keep my tone light while I'm tempted to tell her to fuck right off.

That's a little dramatic.

I clear my throat, silently urging myself to get a grip. It's not Liz's fault my panties are in such a twist. No, that victory lies solely in the hands of the stepbrother I let pull down an entirely different pair last night.

Not thinking about it. I am not *thinking about it.*

"Um, okay, everyone take your seats as quickly as possible, please. We've got a lot to cover today."

As the class settles, I try to shove the flowers to the back of my mind. Easier said than done when they're a looming gargantuan spectacle in the middle of my classroom. They have to be from Dom. Some misguided peace offering, no doubt. What could the note possibly say?

'Sorry for spilling my load inside you, I've realized that's a pretty weird thing for a stepbrother to do. Let's forget the whole thing ever happened?'

I shove the arrangement to the corner of my desk, determined not to let him throw me off balance when the day has barely begun. The last thing I want to think about today is the role *I* played in the whole twisted mess.

The morning flies by in a flurry of Shakespeare quotes and grammar exercises. When the lunch bell rings I find myself alone in the classroom once again, staring at the damn flowers. Curiosity finally gets the better of me, and I pluck out the small envelope nestled among the blooms.

My fingers tremble slightly as I tear it open, bracing myself for whatever snarky message Dom's left for me. But as I unfold the card, I'm met with...*nothing*. It's completely blank. No name, no message, not even a florist's logo.

A chill runs down my spine. This isn't Dom's style at all. He'd never miss an opportunity to be smug or take credit for fucking with my head. So, who the hell sent these?

I'm still frowning at the empty card when a voice startles me back to reality. "Earth to Shiloh! You coming to lunch or what?"

I look up to see Luke leaning against the doorframe, his massive arms crossed over his chest and one blonde eyebrow raised comically high. "Sorry, yeah, I let myself get distracted. I'm coming now."

I tuck the card into my pocket and follow him to the teacher's lounge, where the rest of our little group is already gathered. As soon as I sit down, I'm met with knowing grins.

"So," Ruby leans in. "Spill it immediately. Who's the lucky guy?"

I blink, my mind as blank as that infernal card. "What?"

"Oh, come on," she giggles. "The flowers? Half the school's talking about it already."

"Oh, I... I don't know," I admit, pulling out my sad excuse for a lunch–a slightly squashed peanut butter sandwich I threw together in my haste to leave the house this morning. "There wasn't a card."

This response elicits a chorus of intrigued "*Ooh*"s from the group. I take a bite of my sandwich to avoid having to say more.

"Maybe you've got yourself a secret admirer," Luke wiggles his eyebrows suggestively, causing Greyson to punch him playfully in the bicep. "About time, if you ask me. How long has it been since you've been on a date, anyway?"

I nearly choke on my mouthful of sticky bread. If they only knew what–or rather *who*–I'd done last night. But that thought only makes me feel nauseated. These are my friends. I should be able to tell them anything. And yet, that's a secret I'll be taking to my grave.

"I'm not holding out for some mystery man," I finally manage. "Or any man, for that matter. I'm perfectly happy with my quiet little life here, and my books."

"Amen to that," Jemma pipes up. I can always count on her to echo such a sentiment.

The conversation mercifully shifts to other topics, the group clearly sensing my less-than-gleeful outlook on the whole subject. But my mind keeps wandering back, keeping me from fully hearing the conversation. The unanswered questions nag at me the entire lunch hour, until I'm convinced I'm losing my mind all over again.

As the bell signals the start of the next period, I hurriedly gather my things and power walk back to my classroom. As I lecture about the symbolism in "*The Great Gatsby*," my eyes keep darting to the gratuitous arrangement. While its cloying scent permeates the room, I can't help but think of the cloaked figure at Fairchild Manor. If some prankster out there is determined to fuck with me, they're getting exactly what they want.

And if it's not Dom, what the fuck did I do to deserve two psychos on my ass?

I catch a few students exchanging curious glances and have to resist the urge to snap at them that I'm *totally fucking fine.* I force myself to focus on Fitzgerald's prose, on the green light at the end of Daisy's dock–on anything but those damn flowers.

By the time the final bell rings, I'm mentally and emotionally exhausted. I slump into my chair as the last student files out, rubbing my temples to ward off an impending headache. The bouquet still mocks me from its perch, the vibrant colors a stark contrast to my stormy mood.

With a sigh, I start packing up my things. As much as I'd love to leave the arrangement here and deal with it tomorrow, I know the rumors would only run wild if it looked like I was rejecting the gift. Reluctantly, I gather the vase in my arms, casting one last glance around the classroom before flicking off the lights. I'm certain they'd look much better decorating the inside of my trash can.

The cool evening air hits my flushed face as I step into the parking lot, a welcome relief after a day in a stuffy classroom filled with nosy teenagers. My arms already ache from carrying the flowers this far, and I can't wait to be rid of them and sit back with a much-needed glass of wine. Despite what Dom may think, I don't have an alcohol problem. But I do seem to have a problem with unwanted attention.

I fumble for my keys, barely managing to juggle the vase and my book-laden bag. Finally, I manage to unlock the car and chuck the flowers on the passenger seat. With a sigh of relief, I slide behind the wheel, ready to put this place in my rearview.

I turn the key in the ignition. Nothing happens. Frowning, I try again. The engine sputters weakly but refuses to turn over. "Come on, you piece of junk," I mutter, giving it one more attempt. Still nothing.

Frustration bubbles up inside me as I pop the hood and climb out of the car.

Could things really get any worse?

I stare at the engine, quickly realizing I have no clue what I'm supposed to be looking at. Looking around for any kind of small miracle, I find the parking lot is deserted. Because, of course, this would happen to me on the day I'm the last to leave.

"Shit," I curse under my breath, slamming the hood shut. I lean against the car, pulling out my phone to call for reinforcements. Greyson's number is at the top of my favorites list, and I tap it impatiently.

It rings once, twice, then goes to voicemail. "Hey, it's Greyson. Leave a message."

"Hey man, are you busy? My car won't start, and I'm stuck at school. Call me back ASAP, please!"

I end the call and immediately dial my dad's number next. It rings and rings, but still, no one picks up. I leave another desperate message, the slight crack in my voice betraying my growing frustration.

As I lower the phone again, the reality of my situation sinks in. I'm alone in an empty parking lot, with a useless car and a very long walk home. I silently curse myself for not buying a house closer to the high school. The sun is setting, casting long shadows across the asphalt, and an involuntary shiver wracks my spine.

I glance back down at my phone screen, thumb still hovering over the contacts list. There's one more person I could call, but the thought makes my stomach churn. Asking Dom for help would feel like admitting defeat, like proving him right about me wanting him around.

I pace back and forth for a few minutes, weighing my options. I could wait here and hope someone shows up, but there's no way of knowing if that could happen before the morning. I could try walking, but it's miles to my house and the sunlight is rapidly disappearing.

"Fuck it," I mutter, hitting Dom's number before I can remind myself of all the reasons it's a terrible idea.

A shock to absolutely no one, he's the person who picks up on the second ring. "Well, this is a surprise... Miss me already?"

His taunting tone immediately sets my teeth on edge. "Don't flatter yourself," I snap. "Look, I wouldn't be calling if I had any other choice. My car won't start, and I'm stuck at school. Can you...can you come pick me up?"

There's a long pause, and I can practically hear his smug smile. "Now why would I want to do that? Will there be a goodnight kiss in it for me?"

I close my eyes, swallowing my pride along with a not-so-healthy dose of acidic shame. "Please, Dom. I've had a really long day, and I just want to go home."

Another pause. "Fine. I'll be there in ten minutes. Try not to freeze to death before I arrive."

The line goes dead before I can respond. I shove my phone back in my bag and wrap my arms tightly around myself, relief and dread swirling in my stomach.

The next ten minutes feel like an eternity. I pace the parking lot, checking the time obsessively. I think about the flowers, still sitting discarded in my useless car. Dom didn't mention them on the phone. If he had sent them, surely, he would be demanding my simpering gratitude.

The conversation from lunch keeps replaying in my head. A secret admirer? If only my friends knew the truth–that the only man occupying my thoughts right now is my insuffer-able stepbrother who just happens to have given me the best orgasm of my life.

As the sky darkens to a deep indigo, headlights appear at the entrance to the parking lot. My heart rate picks up as Dom's sleek black car pulls up beside me, the engine purring smoothly before he cuts it off.

He steps out, looking annoyingly put-together as usual in a crisp white shirt and dark slacks. His eyes rake over me slowly, taking in my disheveled appearance. "Rough day, Teach?"

I bite back a scathing retort, no doubt he'd love to see me

riled again so soon. "Can we just go? I'd like to salvage what's left of my evening."

He holds up his hands in mock surrender. "By all means. Your chariot awaits."

I hesitate for a moment, staring at the car. Getting in feels like crossing a line, like opening myself up to whatever game Dom's playing. But as a biting wind whips through the parking lot, I realize I don't have much choice.

16

DOMINIC

DESPITE MY PERFECTLY NICE INVITATION, Shiloh doesn't immediately move to climb into my passenger seat. Instead, she remains stubbornly in place, arms crossed tightly over her chest.

"Is this standoff going to last much longer? I'm bored already," I sigh, folding my own arms to imitate her defensive posture.

Her eyes narrow to thin slits, "I'm just deciding whether standing out here all night would actually be preferable to going anywhere with you."

I roll my eyes. I can't help it. The sooner she realizes she's just as obsessed with me as I am with her, the sooner we can be done with this false reluctance. "By all means take your time...What's up with the car anyway?"

"I haven't got a damn clue," she bites out. "The stupid thing won't start."

"Why don't I take a look at it, while you decide whether or not to sleep here tonight?" I saunter over, relishing every step that brings us closer. As if reading my mind, she instantly moves away, rounding her dead vehicle so that she can pop the hood. While a disappointment, it's fine.

I've already got you closer than you know, Shy Girl.

"Hmm." I make a brief show of examining the engine. All I have to do is tinker with a few things and it's easy enough to convince a clueless Shiloh that I'm conducting a thorough investigation.

"Alright," she huffs. "Professor Gadget, do you know what the problem is or not?"

"Looks to me like your battery is dead." I have to dip my head low to conceal my smirk as I reconnect the cable to her alternator that I may or may not have disconnected earlier today. "How old is this thing?" The false innocence in my voice is possibly my best performance to date.

Shiloh's cheeks color slightly as she shifts her weight from foot to foot, avoiding eye contact. "I don't know," she mumbles. "Probably pretty old."

I straighten up, wiping my hands on a handkerchief I've pulled from my pocket. "Well, there's your problem. These things don't last forever, you know."

"Yes, thank you for that invaluable insight, Dominic. I'll be sure to leave you a glowing Yelp review."

It's incredibly hard not to chuckle at her embarrassed snapping, but I manage to hold it back. "Chill, Shy, I wasn't judging. I'll call someone to come out and pick it up."

"No, I can do tha–"

I silence her with a wave of my hand, already holding my phone up to my ear. She simply stands there and scowls while I arrange for a wrecker to come and tow the hunk of shit to their lot for safe keeping. Shiloh watches me the whole time, chewing on her lip again. I grow hard immediately, that enticing habit making me imagine the things we could do.

Right here. Right now.

But I brush it off–being the good brother I am. "Done," I announce once I've hung up the phone. "Now, get in the car, Shiloh. I'm taking you home."

She stews for a few more seconds, and I can almost see the gears turning in her head. Part of me wonders if she's going to wait for the tow truck, but really, I already know she's going to say yes. She can't resist when I toss her a direct command. That fire in her eyes makes it obvious.

"Fine," she grouses, giving me a wide berth as she pads towards my passenger door. This time the chuckle that rumbles in my chest is unavoidable. Her insistence on keeping as much space between us as possible is all too ironic as she climbs into my passenger seat.

Shiloh stares pointedly out of her window, her knees pressed tightly together and angled away from me as far as the confines of the car will allow. It doesn't bother me one bit. I succeeded in bringing us together again, and close enough that I can smell her berry shampoo.

Were the means a little questionable?

Maybe. But the end result is worth it.

A couple of miles flit by as we sit in the wordless tension. No doubt Shiloh wants to pretend she's successfully icing me out, but personally, I find the whole thing hot as fuck. I'm still mulling over my options for how to shatter that harsh exterior of hers and worm my way back in, when her phone starts buzzing loudly in her purse.

Out of the corner of my eye I watch her fumble with it, her face noticeably paling as she spots the caller ID.

"Shit," she mutters, immediately swiping to answer. "Yeah? Melanie, hi. I know, I'm so sorry, I completely–"

Even without the call on speaker, I can hear the shrill tones of Melanie's voice as if she were in the car with us. Shiloh winces, holding the phone away from her ear like she's nervous about hearing damage.

"Yes, of course... No, I'm on my way now. My car broke down, but I'll be there soon...I'm so–" Shiloh drops the phone into her lap as the line goes dead. She then lets her head fall back with a loud groan. "Fuck, fuck, *fuck*. I forgot about the committee meeting this afternoon at Fairchild Manor. Do you think you could..." Her voice trails off as we *finally* make eye contact.

"Change course? Why, of course." I finish, already signaling to turn. "Can't let Melanie think we're slackers, can we?"

Shiloh eyes me suspiciously as we roll to a stop at a red light. "You're being awfully accommodating today."

I keep my eyes on the road, my expression carefully neutral. "What can I say? You've caught me in a good mood."

She snorts, clearly unconvinced, but doesn't pursue the subject further. I wish she would. I wish she'd give me the opportunity to say that being in the same space as her would be enough to improve even my blackest moods–that what we did last night still has me riding a high I've never felt before.

Maybe someday, I can get it through her thick fucking skull.

~

As we pull up to Fairchild Manor, I can't help but admire the towering structure that used to intrigue me as a teenager. It's the perfect setting for the dark fantasies already forming in my mind. Of course, they all involve a certain little toy with chaotic blonde hair and the most fuckable plump lips...

Who practically *leaps* from my car like it's on fire.

I watch her rush toward the front door, her hurried steps a stark contrast to the eerie stillness of the manor grounds. The bounce of her tempting ass as she runs is almost hypnotic, and I allow myself a moment to imagine chasing her through the winding halls of the old house. It's been too long since we played our addictive game.

Finally, I climb out myself and follow at a more leisurely pace, drinking in the atmosphere and trying not to be too irritated that our trip back to Shiloh's house was interrupted. The crunch of gravel under my feet, the whisper of wind through ancient trees, the faint scent of decay that seems to cling to the entire place–it all adds to this hunger building within me. I'm sure while we're here I could find the opportunity to have some fun.

Inside, the committee meeting is already in full swing. Melanie's grating voice echoes through the cavernous foyer, leading us through to the dining room that's been fashioned for the occasion. Shiloh slips in silently, no doubt trying to blend into the background, but Melanie's hawkish gaze narrows on her immediately.

"So nice of you to finally join us, Shiloh," she simpers, her close-lipped smile making me wonder if she's concealing fangs.

But the moment I step into the room behind my nervous little sister, the atmosphere shifts completely. Melanie's expression morphs from mocking irritation to fawning admiration so quickly I'm surprised she doesn't get whiplash.

"Dominic! I didn't realize you'd be joining us today. How lucky for us all. I can't wait to hear your insights."

My nod is non-committal as I take a seat at the far end of the table. From here, I have a perfect view of Shiloh as she fishes out her notebook and a pen. She's clearly flustered, a light sheen of sweat visible on her chest that makes me want to pin her down and lick it off.

The meeting recommences after our brief interruption and I tune out Melanie's jabbering about ticket sales, focusing instead on Shiloh's subtle reactions. I notice the way she bites her bottom lip when she's thinking hard, the slight furrow of her brow when she disagrees with something but is too polite–or too terrified–to speak up, and of course, the barely perceptible sag in her shoulders when Melanie shoots down yet another of her ideas.

I read her like an open book, and I have to admit, it's one I want to write my name in over and over again until she's unrecognizable as anything but mine. I want her to be *branded* with me, so that the whole fucking world knows it, too.

What an upheaval I'd be willing to make for you, Shy Girl.

If Shy notices me staring, she doesn't react. Instead, she looks as if she's trying to muster the courage to speak up again, her mouth opening and closing several times as she fails to find a gap in Melanie's latest monologue.

"If it will help Peter with designing new posters, I'd be happy to share my thoughts on the decorations," she finally pipes up, clearing her throat when her words come out a little raspy. "I was thinking we could tie some witchy elements in with the masked theme. You know, to really play up the history of the Manor grounds. I mean, what could be more macabre than our very own stories of witch burnings and black magic?"

As Shiloh elaborates on her vision to a rapt audience, I can't help but let my mind wander. I picture her in a flowing black gown that hugs her waist, and an intricate mask obscuring half her face as she glances back over her shoulder. She's running from me through the dimly lit halls of this house, her breath coming in quick pants. But she'll never escape me, I'm *right* behind her, heady adrenaline coursing through my veins as I chase her down.

In my fantasy, I eventually catch her at the end of a long, dark corridor with no exits. She struggles against my hold, but it's half hearted at best. We've played this game too many times for her to convince me she actually wants to escape. I crowd her against the wall, my body pressed flush to hers as I pin her wrists to the peeling wallpaper above her head. I can almost feel the heat of her skin, and taste the fear and excitement on her lips as I claim them with my own.

"Oh, I *love* it!" someone suddenly exclaims, interrupting my daydream. I quickly refocus my eyes to catch sight of the librarian, Jemma, I think, clapping an encouraging hand on Shiloh's shoulder. Her enthusiasm is a stark contrast to Melanie's barely concealed disdain. "I actually have some catering ideas that would fit perfectly with Shiloh's plan."

I lean back in my chair, content to watch this dynamic unfold as Shiloh's spirits visibly lift right in front of me. Before Melanie can interject, Jemma quickly launches into a detailed description of her own proposal, which seems to revolve around traditional New England fare with a Halloween twist.

"And for the pièce de résistance," she announces, grinning with obvious excitement, "I thought we could roast a whole hog on a spit outside. It would add this awesome fire element to the event, and really play up the witch hunt angle."

As the debate picks up around the table, my imagination takes off once again. This time, I picture Shiloh trussed up before me, suspended and helpless. In my mind, I circle her slowly, drinking in every inch of her exposed flesh, completely vulnerable to me. I can almost hear her whimpers, see the fear and arousal in her glistening eyes as I decide exactly what to do with her.

The vision is so vivid I have to shift in my seat, grateful for the large table hiding my rapidly hardening cock. I force myself to pay attention to the conversation, pushing the fantasy to the back of my mind.

For now.

Melanie looks like she's chewing on a lemon, her lips pursed in obvious displeasure at the direction the meeting has taken. She turns to me, plastering a saccharine smile on her face.

"Well, Dominic," she simpers, "what are your thoughts? I'm sure you must have some concerns about the...*theatrical* nature of these suggestions."

I can see Shiloh tense up out of the corner of my eye, clearly expecting me to tear apart her ideas in front of the entire group...

But I have a different game in mind.

"Actually," I drawl, affecting a tone of bored indifference,

"I think these two have come up with some rather interesting concepts. It's refreshing to see people thinking outside the box. Lord knows dull masquerade themes have been done to death."

Melanie's jaw drops slightly before she catches herself. Shiloh looks equally shocked, her eyebrows shooting up towards her hairline.

"It's a good thing you have me as your sponsor," I continue, "pulling off something this ambitious will require a significant budget. And seeing as we're representing Black-wood Enterprises, I want this to be an event people talk about for years to come."

Excited murmurs ripple around the table. Melanie looks hilariously pained, like she's trying to shove those fangs back up into her gums through sheer willpower. Meanwhile, Jemma is practically bouncing out of her seat–but, of course, it's Shiloh's reaction that interests me most.

She's watching me warily, her eyes narrowed in clear suspicion. I gladly return her gaze, allowing a satisfied smirk to play at the corner of my mouth while I pour every ounce of my desire, my dark intentions, into that look. I want her to *feel* it, to understand on a primal level that she's well and truly trapped within my sights.

Shiloh's eyes widen almost imperceptibly, a pink flush creeping up her face before she quickly looks away. But it's enough. I've seen it. That flicker of realization...of *intrigue.*

A wider, teeth-baring grin spreads across my face as Melanie grudgingly brings the meeting to a close and I slowly rise from my seat. The game is on, and Shiloh is well aware just how much I love to win.

17

SHILOH

As everyone begins to gather their things, Cornelius appears from Lord Knows Where, an ancient set of keys jingling in his hand.

"For you, Miss Wilson," he chimes merrily, dropping them into my palm. "You are welcome to drop by whenever you're ready to make a start on your decorating plans. I'm afraid I won't be much help with the finesse of it all, but I'll be sure to convene with the spirits so that you can work without any hindrance from them."

I choose to smile graciously rather than comment on his bizarre offer of support. "Thanks, Cornelius. I'll do my best not to, um, let them down."

"I'm sure you'll do a wonderful job, dear child," he beams. "You'll see over in the corner there I've brought out several boxes of old bits and pieces that decorated our illustrious venue in days gone by. I must tell you, Old Prudence *loved* the year we had a black and red theme, the predictable old maid." A distant look fills his eyes for a moment, and then he visibly twitches. "Alrighty then, I'll be heading home." With that, he dawdles off, muttering to invisible figures with the occasional conspiratorial cackle.

While the rest of the group files out, I turn toward the dusty boxes, surprised to see Dom lingering behind. He's rifling through one, seemingly absorbed in the task. I try to ignore the prickle of awareness that crawls up my spine as we're suddenly left completely alone.

The silence between us is heavy, charged with an energy I can't quite name. I want to thank him for supporting me in the meeting, but the words stick in my throat. I catch myself stealing glances at him, watching the way his hands move deftly through the box with a slight furrow of concentration between his brows. Try as I might, I still can't put my finger on why he's suddenly so committed to making our trivial event a resounding success.

It's so out of character, I might accuse him of being possessed.

As I watch, thoroughly distracted from sorting through my own box, Dom pulls something dark from the depths of his. I stare transfixed as he turns an ornate mask over in his hands. It appears to be a wolf's head fashioned out of black lace with glinting metallic teeth. Without a word, he slips it on, obscuring the top half of his face. My breath catches at the sight of him, taking in the mysterious and somehow seemingly more dangerous persona it gives him. It's as if the last of his humanity has suddenly been locked away, revealing the beast within.

He reaches back into the box and pulls out a fake meat cleaver, the plastic blade dull in the low light of the room.

When he speaks, his voice drops an octave from his usual mocking timbre, making the hairs on the back of my neck stand on end.

"Do you remember that game we used to play, Shy Girl? *Run and Hide*?"

I can't contain the nervous laugh that escapes me. "You can't be for real. We're not kids anymore, Dom."

But there's something in the way he's standing, in the predatory tilt of his head, that tells me he's far from joking. My heart begins to race, torn between allegiance to the voice in my head screaming *this is ridiculous* and the primal instinct in my gut urging me to flee.

"Dom, we shouldn't..." I begin, but the words die on my tongue as he takes a slow step toward me. It's a clear, imposing warning—one that leaves chills raking down my spine.

"What's the matter, Shy? Afraid you can't resist me?" he taunts, flashing his gleaming teeth beneath the jaws of the wolf. "Let's *play*."

And just like that, he lunges and I'm running. My feet carry me out of the room and down the winding hallways of the Manor before I can even conjure a rational thought. I hear Dom's steady footsteps behind me, unhurried but relentless, as if he knows he has all the time in the world to track me down.

I can't believe we're doing this right now.

But I also can't believe I feel so fucking alive.

The sprawling house is a maze of shadows and cobwebs, the fading afternoon light casting eerie patterns through the dusty windows. I skid around corners and dash through doorways, my breath coming in ragged gasps. All the while, I can feel Dom behind me, his pace never faltering. I know he could've caught me by now, and the fact that he's prolonging it only serves to frighten me further.

I finally burst through a set of double doors at the end of another corridor and find myself in the library. Rows upon rows of bookshelves tower around me, the musty scent of old paper filling my nostrils. Without hesitating for a second, I weave between the stacks, hoping to lose Dom in the labyrinth and circle back to freedom.

But as I round the corner of another shelf, I suddenly find myself face to face with a dead end. Cursing under my breath, I spin around, trying to remember which direction will lead me out again. Just as I pause to wipe the sweat from my brow, I gasp.

He's right there. And blocking my escape.

Dom advances slowly, deliberately, like a predator who knows his prey is cornered and utterly helpless.

With careful steps, I back up until I feel the hard press of the bookshelf against my spine. My breaths grow increasingly laborious with anticipation, and Dom keeps coming, not stopping until he's mere inches away from me. He lingers there, leaving me to feel the heat radiating off his body, and smell the faint scent of his cologne mingling with the musk of sweat from our chase.

"Nowhere left to run, little sis," he purrs, placing his hands on the shelf either side of my head so that I'm caged within his arms.

"We can't do this here," I protest weakly, my eyes darting to the stacks behind him as I try to remember where the damn door is. "Someone could come back…"

"You had better be quiet then," Dom says, running the stupid fake cleaver along my jaw. He drops it to the floor and then peels the mask off his face. It lands beside the cleaver, and as I look back up to him, I'm pinned under the full weight of his dark gaze.

I part my lips, my brain screaming to protest.

But I *can't* force the words out.

Dom lunges forward and bites down on my lower lip, not hard enough to draw blood but with enough force to make me whimper. He seizes the opportunity to sweep his tongue into my mouth, tasting, exploring, demanding a response that I'm helpless to deny him.

I crumble against him, my body betraying me once again even as my mind screams that I should put an end to this. My hands clench around the open front of his jacket–whether to push him away or pull him closer, I'm not sure. All I can think about is the fierce dominance of his mouth on mine, the solid press of his body against me, and the dizzying rush of desire that's coursing through my veins.

He devours me until I'm pounding my fist against his chest, begging for air. And when Dom finally releases my lips, we're both panting.

He leans in, his murmur a shock to my system. "Tell me you don't want this, Shy Girl. I dare you."

"I..." My voice trails off, morphing to a defeated whimper as his lips brush my neck.

"*Tell me,*" he whispers. It's so uncharacteristic of him, and it shatters my fucking walls like a violent, murderous grenade.

I want this.

God help me, I want *him* so bad it hurts.

Finally, I manage to catch his gaze, and say the three words. "I want you."

Dom's low chuckle sends a molten heat licking down my spine. "That's what I thought. You can't resist me any more than I can resist you."

His lips crash down on mine again, and I surrender completely to the tide of desire that threatens to drown us both. Dom grinds into me where I'm trapped against the stacks of books, his arousal evident through his slacks. I can't help but respond, my hips arching into his, driven by instinct alone. He growls low in his throat, the hungry sound vibrating through me and igniting a fire deep in my core.

"So eager for me already," he murmurs, every word dripping with smug victory. I bite my lip, unwilling to admit how right he is. But the evidence will be only too obvious soon enough, we both know where this is going.

Dom's smirk is reminiscent of the Devil himself as he sinks to his knees before me, his near-black eyes never leaving mine. In one fluid motion, he throws my leg over his shoulder, pushing my skirt up around my waist with his other hand. I gasp at the sudden exposure, cool air hitting my flushed skin. Dom wastes no time, immediately hooking his fingers into my soaked panties and dragging them to the side.

"Fuck," he breathes, finally releasing me from his gaze as his eyes drop to my bared pussy. "I'll never get enough of seeing your pretty little cunt weep for me."

He leans in, scraping his teeth over my clit. The sharp pain quickly dissolves into pleasure so intense I have to bite back a scream, my hands scrabbling for purchase on the bookshelves behind me. Dom doesn't hold back, diving in with a fervor that I've never seen in any man knelt between my legs. His tongue laves over my slit, swirling through my pooling arousal before licking up to focus on my clit. He pulls the sensitive bud into his mouth, alternating between sucking hard and quick flicks of his tongue that have my eyes rolling into the back of my head.

I'm vaguely aware that I'm making far too much noise—gasps, yelps, and deep moans I couldn't control even if I tried. Dom's strong hands grip my thighs, holding me right where he wants me as he devours my pussy like a starving man at a lavish feast.

But just as I feel myself teetering on the edge of release and my legs trembling with the effort of staying upright, he pulls away. I can't hold back the disappointed whine that bursts from my lips, my hips chasing his mouth on a reflex.

I'm so fucking hungry for more.

Dom's glistening lips tilt in that ever-present smirk as he rises to his feet with a grace that shouldn't be possible after kneeling on the hard floor for so long. He bends down to brush his lips over mine again, forcing me to taste myself on him. The kiss is surprisingly gentle, a million miles from the hungry intensity just moments before.

"You taste fucking divine," he murmurs against my lips. "I could do it for hours."

My cheeks flame at his words, butterflies swarming in my stomach at the praise. Dom's hands slide up my sides again until he pushes my cardigan off my shoulders. Once it falls to the floor, he strokes his fingertips back up my arms like he's intent on worshiping every inch of my skin. The tender exploration has my heart sputtering until I'm convinced it's about to stop altogether.

Once he reaches my shoulders again, he tugs the straps

of my camisole and bra down roughly, leaving them both bunched around my waist just like he did with my skirt. The move effectively traps my arms, pinning them to my sides.

"Mmm, I do enjoy the sight of you all tied up for me," Dom purrs, his dark eyes raking over my bare chest.

I should feel self-conscious, standing here half-naked and completely at his mercy. But the hunger in his gaze as he drinks in the sight of me has me feeling more desired than I ever have before. He raises his hands to brush his knuckles over my nipples, both of them already pebbled from the cold–and just how fucking turned on I am right now. I arch towards his touch, a breathy moan escaping me as our eyes lock onto each other again.

He leans in slowly as I watch, replacing one hand with his mouth. The wet heat of his tongue circling my nipple draws another whimper from me, my head falling back against the bookshelf with a dull thud as my eyes flutter closed.

"So sensitive," Dom muses, pulling back just enough to blow cool air over the slick skin. I shiver, the goosebumps erupting all over my body. "Look at you, my little Shy Girl. So fucking beautiful."

His words have a hard lump forming in my throat, sending those traitorous butterflies fluttering from my stomach straight up into my chest. My heart hammers wildly, this stolen moment suddenly feeling a lot less like a harmless game.

I'm terrified by how badly I want this–want him. With Dom's greedy hands on my body and his praise ringing in my ears, I can't bring myself to care that he's supposed to be a brother to me. Every second we spend like this, lost in each other, the butterflies in my chest only multiply, their wings beating a frantic rhythm that matches the throbbing between my thighs.

Am I... Am I falling *for him?*

Before I can think it through, I'm drowning again.

Lost to the forbidden thrill of it all.

18

DOMINIC

"Please, Dom," Shiloh gasps against my lips. "I want you to fuck me."

The sound of her breathless plea sends a bolt of pure lightning through my body. My cock throbs painfully in my slacks as she grinds her hips into me again. I've never felt more powerful, or more alive than I do hearing those words fall from her lips.

I scoop her up into my arms, more than happy to give her exactly what she wants. She's so light I can't help but think about how fragile she is, warm and boneless against my chest. I stride purposefully back through the maze of bookshelves, looking for a convenient place to ruin her. The space soon opens up into a vacant reading area, an empty table in the center. It looks like sturdy oak, probably as old as this godforsaken manor.

I will enjoy defiling it.

I lay Shiloh down, relishing the way she immediately gasps at the edge of the wood. Her arms are still trapped at her sides by her bunched-up clothes, as if she's a gift I only bothered to partially unwrap in my rush to claim her. She spreads her legs without bothering to say another word, a silent invitation I'm ready to take full advantage of.

The rush of victory is so intense, I have to pause for a moment. My balls are already tightening, ready to blow my load right into my pants... But I refuse to let this end too quickly. I'm going to savor every fucking second. She asked for it this time, and I need to hear it again.

I free my aching cock from my slacks, hissing at the sensation as cool air hits burning flesh. I pump it leisurely, once, twice, three times, watching Shiloh's hungry eyes follow the movement. Her tongue darts out to wet her rosy lips and the sight is almost my total defeat.

Determined to draw this out, I drag the head of my cock against her entrance with tortuous slowness. Her panties are still bunched to the side, forcing her pussy lips to pucker for me. Shiloh moans with obvious frustration, her hips lifting off the table in a desperate bid for more.

"Don't tease me," she whimpers, fingers clenching and unclenching over the wood beneath her.

I smirk, basking in her newfound desperation. "Beg for it again," I command. "Tell me exactly what you want, little sis."

Shiloh's bright eyes flash with something I can't quite identify–defiance, maybe, or shame–but it's quickly overwhelmed by powerful lust. "Please," she whines. "I need you inside me, Dom. Fuck me hard."

A satisfied growl tears from my throat as I finally, *finally* sink into her tight heat. The sensation is indescribable, like the most addictive drug I'd hit again and again even if it threatened to kill me. Her sweet cunt envelops me like a glove. I pull out of her completely just to relive the feeling of plunging back in all over again. Soon enough, I can't hold back any longer, I begin pounding into her hips at a punishing pace that has us both groaning raggedly.

The table creaks dangerously beneath her, the legs wobbling with each powerful thrust I drive into her hips. Shiloh drops her head back as her moans fill the cavernous room, echoing off the high ceiling and row after row of dusty tomes. I find myself secretly hoping someone *will* stumble upon us. Let them see that I've won, and how fucking thoroughly I'm claiming my prize.

I hook my hands under Shiloh's knees and push them up to her chest. The new angle lets me sink even deeper, and my eyes almost fall closed at the feeling of her clenching around me. However, I don't want to lose sight of her face. I want to watch every moment of what this is doing to her. I want to fuck her so ravenously she'll feel me for days, weeks even. I want her to think of nothing but this moment every time she tries to sit down.

When I'm dangerously close to spilling inside her, I reach between us to stroke over her clit with my thumb. Shiloh's eyes fly open again, her desperate gaze finding mine as I drag every last ounce of pleasure out of her.

"Come for me, baby," I demand. "I want to watch you fall apart."

I drink in every detail of her face as she shatters beneath me. The flutter of her eyelashes when her eyes roll back, the deepening flush in her cheeks as she stops breathing for a moment, the way her lips fall open on a silent cry have me in complete and total awe.

Having a front row seat to her orgasm is nothing short of transcendent. My heart clenches in my chest while her pussy clenches on my dick. A surge of possessive pride mingles with something deeper, more dangerous–something that I don't care to name. Before I can examine the feeling too closely, my own release crashes into me. I bury myself as deep as I can, filling Shiloh with pulse after pulse of hot cum.

For a few triumphant moments, the only sound within these walls is our ragged breathing. I allow myself a handful of seconds to admire the rise and fall of Shiloh's naked breasts before I pull out of her, eager to see the evidence I've left behind.

My cum seeps from her puffy, blushing cunt, and the sight nearly makes me hard all over again. I swipe through the mess with my fingers before pushing it back inside her and tugging the fabric of her panties back into place. "I want you full of me always," I murmur, though it's more to myself than to her.

If she hears me, Shiloh doesn't respond. She just lies still, staring up at the ceiling with a dazed expression while I gently lower her knees back to the table. I tuck myself back into my slacks, admiring the view for as long as she'll let me.

When I return from retrieving her cardigan around the corner, she still hasn't moved, and I have to stifle a low chuckle. She looks thoroughly fucked, and the animalistic part of my soul preens at the knowledge I'm the one who reduced her to this state.

I help her sit up slowly, carefully righting her clothes until her chest is covered and her cardigan is draped over her shoulders. She remains quiet as I take her hand, lead her back through the house and out to the car, seemingly lost in her own world.

As I slide into the driver's seat, I can't fight the urge to know what's going through that pretty little head of hers any longer. Her face is a careful mask of contemplation, brow furrowed slightly as she stares out the window.

"Tell me what you're thinking." Shiloh jumps a little when I speak, as if she'd forgotten I was here at all.

She takes a deep breath before answering. "I don't know... You and me? It's just...it's just a lot to process," she says softly. "I can't shake the feeling this is all so wrong. I don't want to be, but I guess I'm a little ashamed."

My grip tightens on the steering wheel enough that my knuckles turn a stark white. "Why is it wrong?" I counter, unable to keep the sharp edge from my voice. "We're not *actually* related. It's not some gross crime for us to want each other. It's not incest."

She turns to look at me then, her wary eyes searching mine, for what, I can't be sure. "You have a point," she eventually relents... But I can still see the conflict swirling in those pale blue depths.

I want to reach out and touch her again, to pull her close and chase away all her doubts. But something in her posture keeps me at bay. She's curled in on herself, arms wrapped around her body as if she's back on the defensive. Arguing the point further would only have her locking down, she needs to come to terms with this on her own.

I sure as fuck won't let it be over though.

The rest of the drive passes in tense silence once again. I rack my brain for something to say, some way to pull her back from whatever turmoil she's trapped in.

Once we pull up to Shiloh's house, I kill the engine and turn to face her fully. "Let's go inside," I say, already reaching for my seatbelt. "I'm sure I know a few ways to wipe that tortured look off your face."

She shakes her head, reaching for the door handle without looking at me. "Not tonight, Dom. I'm tired and... *confused.* I just need to go to bed."

Frustration surges up in my chest, laced with bitter panic. "You're too in your head, Shy. Don't talk yourself out of this like you don't want it as much as I–"

"Not now," she cuts me off, her voice firm despite its distant softness. "*Please*, I just need some time to think."

I grind my teeth together, swallowing the fierce urge to argue. She's slipping away from me, I can feel it. I force myself to nod silently, to accept her decision even as every cell in my body rebels against it.

Shiloh opens the car door, pausing before she steps out. "Thank you for the flowers, by the way," she murmurs, a ghost of a smile lifting her lips. "They're probably all wilted in my car by now, but they were beautiful."

Before I can answer her, she's out of the car and heading up the short path to her door. I watch her go, confusion warring with the lingering desire to follow her inside.

What fucking flowers?

I never sent her any flowers.

The realization hits me like a punch to the gut. Someone else is vying for her attention, trying to win what's already mine. The thought of another man's hands on her, another man's lips against her skin... Fuck, it makes my blood boil. My hands clench to fists in my lap, and I stay parked long after Shiloh has disappeared inside the house, my mind racing.

Those flowers...Who the hell sent them? And more importantly, how am I going to make sure they're the last gift Shiloh ever receives from another man?

19

SHILOH

I PULL into the gravel driveway of Fairchild Manor on Friday evening, the tires of my recently resuscitated car crunching to a halt. It mysteriously showed back up to my house the morning after Dom and I soiled the library's table, and while I was expecting my stepbrother to be with it... He was strikingly absent.

And that's how he's remained for a full week now.

Fishing out my phone, I pull up a message thread to him, my eyes flicking between my screen and the massive manor. I type out the first text I've sent him since that night, and hit the send button, wondering how Dom will take it.

> ME: YOU MISSED THE MEETING. MELANIE
> ORDERED US TO START DECORATING TONIGHT.
> IT'D BE NICE TO HAVE SOME HELP.

Honestly, I wasn't surprised that Dom was a no show tonight. I hadn't really expected him to be there, since I hadn't come crawling back to him. Melanie, on the other hand, seemed noticeably dulled by his lack of presence. Of course, she managed to cheer herself up at the end by insisting I come here and spend my evening decorating.

"I'll need a good idea of what the final product will look like well in advance, Shiloh. Just in case I need to make any adjustments." The glint in her eye as she'd delivered her orders had me dying to make *adjustments* to her smug face.

Ugh. As I kill the engine of my car, my phone buzzes from its perch in the cup holder. Lo and behold, it's a text from my vanished stepbrother.

DOM: START WITHOUT ME.

Great. So...does that mean he's coming?

I grimace, pausing for a moment as I rake my fingers through my already-tousled blonde hair. I grab a hair tie from my console and pull it up into a messy bun on my head. I can't help but wonder what version of Dom I'll get tonight if he shows. Will the space I took turn him back into the demeaning asshole? Or will he still have that strangely appealing soft side?

It doesn't matter. I sigh at the thought of his smug face before pocketing my phone and grabbing several garlands of dried herbs from the passenger seat. The sun is already dipping below the tree line, casting long shadows across the overgrown grounds. A shiver rolls down my spine, and I'm fairly certain it has nothing to do with the frigid October air.

The heavy iron keys feel awkward in my hand as I sidle up to the front porch. It takes some wrangling, but eventually the ancient lock gives way with a loud *click*. I push the door open, wincing at the eerie creak of the old hinges. Without Cornelius clowning around, the creepy atmosphere of this place suddenly feels a lot less comical.

The dark entrance hall swallows me whole as I step inside, my fingers fumbling for the nearest light switch. My footsteps echo off the marble floor, every sound almost deafening in the still space. I've been in this house more times than I could count, but being here utterly alone as night falls? Yeah, that has me desperate to run back to the safety of my car and put the whole estate firmly in my rearview.

I do my best to shake off the unease and square my shoulders as I make my way to the ballroom. There's work to be done, and I'll be damned if I give Melanie any more reasons to criticize me. The sooner I get started, the sooner I can get the fuck out of here.

With preparations in full swing, the ballroom is now a mess of half-unpacked boxes and bubble-wrapped vases. I set my bag down with a huff and try to decide where to start. Whoever thought that twenty-foot ceilings were a good idea clearly never had to decorate the damn place.

"Gross fucking cobwebs," I mutter, stretching as far as I can from the top of a rickety ladder Cornelius has kindly left for my use. I'm half convinced he's hoping to add another ghost to his gaggle of unearthly *friends,* given the absolute death-trap I'm currently teetering on. My fingertips just barely graze the nail where I'm trying to hang a garland of ivy. Maybe if I just... reach... a little... further...

The ladder wobbles dangerously. With nothing to grab onto, I'm soon falling backwards with a horrified yelp. I land hard on my ass, my dignity bruised just as badly as my tailbone. For a moment, I just lie there in stunned silence. Then, despite myself, I start to laugh.

"Real graceful, Shiloh," I snort, hauling myself to my feet and rubbing at the sore spot. "Lucky you didn't break your fucking neck."

I'm still chuckling as I dust myself off, ready to tackle the decorations more at my level. But suddenly, I hear a loud *clang!* from somewhere upstairs, like metal dropped on stone.

I freeze, every muscle in my body locking tight as my ears strain to hear any other disturbance. Silence stretches for a long moment, and I'm about ready to dismiss it entirely when another sound echoes through the supposedly empty house. This time it's a series of thuds, as if someone is swiping heavy objects onto the carpeted floor above me.

My heart immediately starts to race. Dom implied he was coming, but I'm certain I would have heard the front door creaking open if he'd shown up. *Right?* There shouldn't be anyone else here.

I debate calling Cornelius...or the police. But what would I even say? *'Hi, I heard a noise in the spooky old mansion I'm decorating for a Halloween party'?*

They'd laugh me right out of town. No, I need to investigate this myself. After all, it's probably just a squirrel that found its way through a cracked window.

Yeah. That must be it.

Or maybe I'll meet one of Cornelius's ghost friends.

Forcing my feet to move as a shudder rolls down my body, I creep back out of the ballroom and towards the grand staircase in the entrance foyer. Each step feels like it takes an eternity, the carpet runner muffling my footsteps as I head up to the second floor. The landing is cloaked in shadow, barely illuminated by the fading twilight outside.

"Hello?" I call out stupidly as I reach the top of the stairs, my voice cracking in my failed attempt to sound confident. "Is someone there?"

The only answer is the groan of old floorboards beneath my feet. I edge down the hallway, intensely aware of every creak and rustle around me. Doors loom on either side, their brass knobs tarnished with age and coated with dust. None of them look disturbed.

So, where the hell did that racket come from?

Suddenly, a floorboard creaks behind me, and I whirl around, my heart in my throat. "Who's there?" I demand, trying desperately to gulp down a full breath. "You can't be in here, this is private property!"

I continue my search on shaky legs. Then, at the far end of the corridor, a shadow moves. I squint, trying to make out details in the gloom. Another few tentative steps forward and I'm certain of what I'm seeing.

The cloaked figure is back, standing starkly still.

I refuse to be frightened again. I decide I'm going to stride right up to the fucker and rip their disguise off Scooby Doo-style. After all, more than likely, it's some student trying to be *spooky*. But, before I can even get halfway down the passage, they turn and dart back the way they came.

"Hey!" I shout, immediately breaking into a run. "Stop!"

I skid around the corner, nearly losing my footing on the worn, holey carpet. The intruder is already disappearing around another bend in the labyrinthine hallways. I'm not giving up, my breath coming in ragged gasps as I sprint like a hound who's caught a scent.

Left, right, another right... I quickly lose track of how many turns we've taken. This manor is a freaking maze, and I'm becoming more disoriented by the second. I round another corner, certain I've finally caught up, only to find myself facing an empty stretch of hallway.

"What the fuck?" I pant, spinning helplessly in a circle. There's no sign of the cloaked figure, and no open doors they may have slipped through. It's like they've vanished into thin air.

I lean against the wall, trying to catch my breath and make sense of what the hell just happened. The house around me has fallen back into eerie silence, no hints reaching my ears of where the figure may have run off to.

Am I losing my damn mind?

I glance around again. Well, one thing's for certain–I have no idea where the hell I am now.

I spin around, trying to get my bearings, but every hallway looks the same in the encroaching darkness. Panic surges up in my chest, threatening to choke me in its iron grip.

"Okay, okay, Shiloh, *think*," I mutter to myself. "Just...retrace your steps and you'll find your way back."

Easier said than done. I start turning corners at random, hoping to find something familiar to tell me I'm heading the right way. With each dead end, my nerves ratchet up another notch. The manor suddenly feels impossibly huge, a black hole designed to swallow me completely. I'm half-convinced I'll be wandering these halls for eternity when a faint glimmer of recognition sparks in my brain.

I swear I've seen that hideous portrait before!

I stare at the painting of some obese, old Fairchild patriarch, his beady eyes seeming to glower right back at me. Yes, I definitely passed this on my way up. Which means...

Relief floods through me as I spot the top of the grand staircase around the next bend. I practically fly down the steps, taking them two at a time in my eagerness to return to familiar territory. In my haste, I slip on the edge of a step near the bottom. I stumble, arms pinwheeling as I frantically fight to regain my balance.

Just as I'm bracing for my second nasty tumble of the evening, I collide with something solid. Strong hands immediately wrap around my biceps, steadying me before I eat shit.

"Whoa there, where's the fire?"

I look up, startled to find myself face-to-face with a bemused-looking Dom. His brow furrows as he takes in my rumpled appearance.

"Shy? What happened? You look like you've seen a ghost."

For maybe half a second, I consider telling him everything. The noises, the chase, the cloaked figure that seemed to vanish into thin air. But even as the words form on my tongue, a creeping doubt has me pressing my lips together. How crazy would I sound, rambling about spooky banging and some phantom intruder? The last thing I need is for Dom to think I'm having a mental breakdown.

He'd no doubt take credit for it.

I force out a laugh that sounds a little hollow even to my own ears. "Oh, nothing, *nothing*. I, uh... I thought I saw a bat fly upstairs. Freaked myself out among all the creepy ass portraits. No biggie."

Dom doesn't look entirely convinced. "If you say so." He pauses, giving me a smirk. "Shall we get this decorating over and done with before we have to spend the whole night here?"

"Yeah, let's." I plaster on what I hope is a winning smile, and he seems content to drop the subject, taking my hand and leading me back towards the ballroom.

I'm surprised to find my racing heart beginning to slow, my frayed nerves settling as if they're being stroked into submission one by one. Even more surprising is the realization it's *Dom's* presence that's soothing me. The warm grip of his hand wrapped around mine.

It's such a casual gesture, but it leaves me reeling. *When did Dominic Blackwood become a source of comfort rather than rampant anxiety?*

Memories of our antagonistic past bubble to the surface of my mind unbidden. The cruel pranks, the scathing remarks, years of animosity and then nothingness stretching between us like a chasm.

And then since he's been back in town...the bickering morphing into actual conversations, the hostile stares melting into heated glances. Oh, and I sure as hell don't know what to make of the downright animalistic sex.

Who is this new Dom? And who the fuck am *I*? None of it makes any sense. Maybe I *am* losing my mind.

And yet, here in this moment, I feel like I could face a hundred phantoms and be confident that the brooding man beside me would have my back.

20

DOMINIC

MY GRIP on the steering wheel is relaxed as I navigate the streets of Avalon, my mind drifting to last night at the manor. I reminisce about how Shiloh's shoulders gradually relaxed as the evening wore on, her laughter becoming less guarded the longer we spent hanging ridiculous bundles of dried herbs and fake cobwebs.

A smirk tugs at my lips as I consider how much faster she recovered from her shame spiral compared to the first time I sank my cock into her. I can feel her coming round to the idea that we're not about to be institutionalized for daring to touch each other. Patience is a virtue, after all.

Granted, I was itching to touch her after half a week of no contact, eager to taste her lips again. But I'm giving her space. I did nothing other than hold her hand. *Once.* She has to see that whatever is growing between us doesn't disappear whenever we keep our clothes on.

It's not like I've been staying away as I wait for her to beg me again, either. I still sneak into her house every night, and still watch her sleep for an hour or so before slipping away to study her journals back in my own room. I've combed those pages so thoroughly anyone would think I was conducting a psychological study on my little Shy Girl.

Knowledge is power. And knowing just how lonely she's been this past decade–how desperate she is just for someone to stand by her and fucking stay there–it's all the information I need to be exactly what she's been yearning for.

Hence, I chose to message her this morning to ask if she wanted to go shopping for costumes. Dressing up for some garish Halloween event is not something I thought I would ever do while I'm still breathing, but I'm certain it's what Shiloh's perfect man would do.

And that's exactly who I intend to be for her. I need her to *need* me.

Pulling up to her house, I take a deep breath before exiting the car. Each step toward her door is a little heavy as I grudgingly realize I actually have to follow through on my promises. Fuck knows what anyone back in New York would say if they heard exactly how Dominic Blackwood is about to spend his Saturday. I rap my knuckles against the chipped paint, pulse quickening despite my best efforts to remain unbothered.

The door swings open barely a minute later, revealing my Shiloh in all her flustered glory. Her hair is chaotic as always, as if she'd been running her fingers through it waiting for me to show up. A light blush already colors her cheeks when she looks up at me.

"Hey," she breathes, eyes darting away again with adorable hesitation.

"Hey yourself," I return, letting my gaze sweep over her

simple jeans and T-shirt. I'll never understand how this woman looks fucking edible in anything. "Ready to go?"

She nods silently, grabbing her coat and purse before locking up. As we walk to the car, I resist the urge to reach out and take her hand. We're not alone in an abandoned house right now, so no doubt beady eyes are on us from all directions.

"So... costume shopping," I say casually as I pull away from the curb. "Any ideas what you're looking for?"

Shiloh shrugs, fiddling nervously with the strap of her bag. "Not really. Something...appropriate, I guess. Um...on theme."

I can't help but snort at her less-than-enthusiastic response. "Appropriate? Come on, Shy Girl, I thought this was your favorite day of the year. Live a little."

She shoots me a glare, but I catch the hint of a smile tugging at the corner of her mouth. "Easy for you to say. You're not the one who's going to be judged when everyone picks apart my theme ideas. If anyone is disappointed, Melanie will throw me straight under the bus."

"True," I concede with a smirk. "But that just means you have to blow them all away with a killer look. Go all out and maybe they'll give you Melanie's job next year."

Shiloh shakes her head with a muted laugh, and we fall into an easy banter as I drive to the other side of town. I find myself stealing glances at her profile every so often, admiring the way the sunlight catches in her golden hair when she turns to look out the window.

Maple Street soon comes into view, a quaint little strip of boutiques and cafes not far from the High School. I park swiftly and round the car to open Shiloh's door, offering my hand to help her out. She hesitates for a split second before taking it, her palm warm against mine.

We head down the sidewalk in easy camaraderie, close enough that our arms occasionally brush. To anyone else, we probably look like two siblings innocently catching up after a long time spent in different States. Shiloh points out various shops, her eyes lighting up as she shares anecdotes about each one.

"And that's where I got my first job in junior year," she says, pointing to a small bookstore. "I'm sure I spent more time reading than actually working. It was awesome."

I chuckle. "Why am I not surprised?"

She elbows me playfully. "Hey man, I'll have you know I was an excellent employee."

"Oh, I'm sure," I tease. "A regular employee of the month, I bet. What were there, like two other teenage competitors?" Her laughter rings out as she shoves me again, leaving my skin burning beneath my clothes where I long for her to never stop touching me.

We eventually come to a stop in front of an eclectic boutique, its window display showcasing an array of elaborate costumes that have definitely seen better days. Shiloh's eyes almost pop out of her face with excitement.

"This is the place," she says, already reaching for the door handle.

A little bell chimes as we enter, and I'm immediately assaulted by the scent of mothballs and stale perfume. Racks upon racks of garish costumes line the walls and create a maze throughout the store.

Shiloh dives in without another word, rifling through the options with childlike glee. It's so cute I struggle to maintain an air of indifference, my instincts screaming at me to just grab her and hold her close. I trail behind her at a safe distance instead, occasionally plucking ridiculous pieces from the racks.

"What about this one?" I ask, holding up a gaudy, sequined monstrosity that might have once been a flamingo costume.

She turns, a shameless cackle bubbling up as soon as she sees it. "Oh hell, no. Hide that thing before someone goes blind."

I grin, shoving it back onto the rack between two equally grotesque options. "Your loss. I think the hideous pink would've suited you perfectly."

Shiloh rolls her eyes, but her easy smile doesn't fade. She continues her hunt undeterred, occasionally holding up other ludicrous eyesores for my opinion. With each comical exchange, I feel the walls she's always trying to maintain between us crumbling brick by brick.

After a while sifting through the circus of bright fabric, Shiloh's arms are laden with potential costumes. I eye the pile skeptically.

"You're gonna need to try those on before you can make an informed decision."

She bites her lip in that addictive way she does when she's unsure of herself. "Um, yeah, is that okay? You can go grab a coffee or something, I know you're probably bored–"

"Nonsense," I cut her off. "This was my idea, wasn't it? Go on, I'll be your captive audience."

Relief washes over her soft features as she grins up at me before disappearing into the nearest changing room. I settle into a chair, preparing myself for what's sure to be an interesting show.

The first few terrible costumes are met with good-natured laughter and teasing critiques. Shiloh twirls in each one, her initial coyness melting away as she gets into the spirit of things. I'm nothing short of stunned to find I'm actually enjoying myself.

"Alright, this one could actually be a contender!" she calls out, eventually stepping from behind the curtain in a sleek, black catsuit.

My eyes rake hungrily over her form, appreciating how the fabric clings to her every curve. "Not bad," I manage, my mouth suddenly dry. "But the black cat thing has been done to death. Chuck it in the 'maybe' pile."

She nods, a knowing look crossing her face before she ducks back into the changing room. I shift in my seat a little, trying to ignore the semi that leapt up at the sight of her in lycra.

"Okay," Shiloh's voice wavers slightly a few minutes later. "I'm not sure about this one, but it's uh...on theme, I guess."

The curtain parts again, and suddenly I can't breathe.

She steps out in a black corseted gown, the silk hugging her waist before tumbling to the floor in a ripple of liquid night. But it's the back–or lack thereof–that has me transfixed. The bust is laced with ribbons that crisscross her spine, leaving a tantalizing expanse of soft, pale skin exposed.

I stand abruptly, unable to resist the urge to get a closer look. Shiloh shifts under my intense gaze, a deep blush blooming across her cheeks and down her neck.

"Well?" she asks nervously. "What do you think? Is it too much?"

I struggle to form any coherent words, my throat tight with a primal hunger I can barely contain. The woman that stands before me is a seductive vision, such a far cry from her usual knitted sweaters and oversized shirts that I'm struck dumb by the sight.

"Uh, Dom?" she prompts, her voice hushed and uncertain. "It's not very *me,* is it?"

I clear my throat, wrestling my brain to function. "It's...perfect," I finally manage, the compliment coming out rougher than I intended. "That's the one. We're getting it."

Shiloh glances back at the mirror behind her, brow furrowed. "But...it's maybe a little too much for me..."

"Nope," I say, perhaps a little too sharply. I soften my tone, reaching for her chin until I can pull her face back to look at me. "It's perfect, Shy. You look incredible. I'm not letting you choose anything else."

She presses her lips together, that familiar war going on behind her eyes. She's fighting the natural instinct to fight me, to try to reclaim some semblance of autonomy. But I know the look too well, and know she loves it when I put my foot down. Finally, Shiloh nods, a sheepish smile smoothing away the lingering doubt. "Alright, fine. You win."

I usher her back into the changing room with a smug grin of my own, needing a moment to remind myself that we're in public and I can't just fuck her over the nearest surface. When she emerges in her regular clothes, gown in hand, I'm only a fraction more composed.

I can't be sure how long that will last.

At the register, I hand over my credit card without hesitation, ignoring Shiloh's weak protests about the extortionate price. Some things are worth every damn penny.

When we step back out onto the street, the crisp autumn air is a welcome respite from the stuffiness inside–and from the hot blood pumping through my body and straight to my crotch. Shiloh turns to me, clutching the garment bag to her chest like a precious relic.

"Dom, I...I don't know what to say," she mumbles, her eyes shining with naked gratitude. "Thank you so much for this. For today. For everything. I don't get it, I don't really understand why you're doing all this, why you're even still in town. But...just, thank you."

The raw confession breaks the last thread of my self-control. I step closer, cupping her warm face in both my hands.

"I'm here because I want to be here. No evil games, Shy, I swear." I stroke my thumbs over her cheekbones, praying she sees the sincerity in my eyes.

Before she can respond, I close the last of the torturous distance between us, capturing her lips with mine. For a heartbeat, Shiloh freezes, and I fear she's about to shove me away all over again. But then she melts against me, her free hand winding around my neck as she returns the kiss with equal fervor.

The world falls away, narrowing to just this moment, just *us*. The taste of her, the soft sounds she makes as I sweep my tongue over hers, and the way her body molds itself to mine– I can't get enough. My hands slide back into her hair, my fingers scraping against her scalp as I grasp her like I'm terrified she might suddenly evaporate.

But then a loud gasp behind me shatters the moment.

We spring apart, both panting heavily. I turn towards the

sound, ready to snap at whatever nosy bystander needs to mind their own fucking business.

But the words die in my throat.

Standing just a few feet away are my mother and Charlie, identically shocked expressions splattered across their faces. Charlie looks like he's been kicked in the balls, his wide eyes darting between Shiloh and me with growing hurt and betrayal. But it's my mother's face that truly chills me–her shock quickly morphing into venomous fury.

"*Dominic,*" she hisses. "What in God's name do you think you're doing?"

Shit. I'd hoped to be better prepared for this moment.

Instinctively, I step in front of Shiloh, shielding her from their accusing glares. "Mother," I start, my mind racing to find a level response that won't give them both a stroke...

Or start a Jerry Springer style feud right here on the sidewalk.

21

SHILOH

Fuck, fuck, fuck, fuck, FUCK! This can't be happening!

My cheeks burn hotter than the sun as I stand paralyzed before our indignant parents. Dom has inched in front of me like a human shield, but I still feel more exposed than that nightmare where you forget to wear clothes to school.

"This is not what it looks like," I blurt out, my voice embarrassingly shrill. "We were just, um…"

"*Actually*, it's exactly what it looks like," Dom interjects smoothly, saving me from having to find something halfway believable to say. His hand slides round to rest on my lower back, a possessive gesture that makes my heart flutter despite the mortification searing through every inch of the rest of me. "Shiloh and I are attracted to each other. We're both consenting adults. There's nothing wrong with what we're doing, so you can wipe those outraged looks off your faces before you cause a scene."

The shock on our parents' faces would almost be comical if I weren't desperately wishing for the ground to open up and swallow me whole. My dad's face has turned an alarming shade of purple by the time he sputters, "Nothing wrong? You're *siblings*, for Christ's sake!"

"*Stepsiblings*. We're not related by blood," Dom argues, his tone maddeningly calm. "And we barely grew up together."

"Regardless, your dad and I are married. Surely you can see how inappropriate this is?" Viv's voice is a strangled rasp as she snaps back, her gaze nervously darting around for fear we have an audience.

"No, I don't," Dom answers firmly. "We haven't been a family in more than a decade–if we ever were. Shiloh and I are nothing more than two people who care about each other."

"This is *insane*," my dad takes a step forward, his voice echoing in the quiet street.

I want to disappear, to rewind time and choose and stay hidden in that changing room for just a few more minutes until the coast was clear. But as Dom's words sink in, *'two people who care about each other,'* a warmth blooms in my abdomen that has absolutely nothing to do with shame.

Suddenly, Dom's fingers close around mine. "I've had enough of this. We're leaving now," he announces, cutting off whatever tirade Viv was about to launch into all over again. "If you can pull your heads out your asses, we might see you at some point. If not, I don't really give a shit."

He pulls me back towards the car, and I follow without resistance, blood pounding in my ears. The defiance in his squared shoulders, the angry set of his jaw–it's all doing things to me that I can't begin to explain right now.

The drive home is deafening silent. I gnaw on my bottom lip while I sneak glances at Dom's profile, admiring the smooth curve of his lips, the muscle that jumps in his cheek as he clenches and unclenches his teeth. I can barely wrap my head around what just happened, everything he said.

Do we really care about each other? Are we more to each other than two lonely people who can't help but fuck occasionally?

"Dom, I..." I start hesitantly, needing to sort this through out loud.

"Not now, Shy," he cuts me off, stern eyes fixed on the road. "I need a minute to calm down."

I nod slowly, settling back into my seat and reliving the way he defended us until a ghost of a smile curves my lips. When we pull up to my house, I turn to Dom with a newfound confidence. "Come inside?"

His eyebrows raise in obvious surprise before nodding wordlessly. Once we get inside, I head straight for the kitchen, desperately seeking something to do with my hands. I pull out two wine glasses, filling them generously with a dark Pinot Noir I bought to recover from our tryst in the library. When I turn back, Dom is leaning against the opposite counter, arms folded tightly over his chest. His posture screams defensive, like he's bracing himself for another fight.

As he opens his mouth, no doubt ready to launch into whatever speech he's been crafting since we climbed into the car, I press a finger to his lips.

"Don't bother," I murmur. "I know what you're thinking, but I'm not about to shriek about the wrongness of it all and kick you out again. Let's just forget we saw them, okay? We don't have to deal with it right now."

Confusion knits his eyebrows together, but he eventually nods. I pick up my wine glass, taking a fortifying gulp before setting it back down with purpose.

This is it. No more avoiding, no more denial.

"Come upstairs with me," I say, lowering my hand to find one of his. His fingers intertwine with mine immediately, as if by instinct. The simple gesture makes my heart stutter. Nothing about it feels wrong.

Too terrified to say another word, I lead him silently upstairs, wishing I'd chugged the entire glass of wine before doing so. By the time we reach my bedroom, nerves threaten to overwhelm me completely. But one look back at Dom–at the intensity in his dark eyes and the way his chest rises and falls with quick breaths–emboldens me to do what I know we're both craving. I step closer, running my palms over his pecs until my fingers find the buttons at his neck. They tremble slightly as I work my way down.

Dom remains still, watching me.

As I push the starched fabric from his shoulders, I can't help but admire every inch of skin I've exposed. It suddenly strikes me how bizarre it is that we've had sex twice and he's never removed an item of clothing. Technically, the only things he's pulled off me have been a pair of panties and a cardigan. Having him here, allowing me to unwrap him like a gift, is a heady thrill I never thought I'd get the chance to chase. My fingertips trace the hard planes of muscle, feeling the warmth of his smooth chest and the steady thump of his heart.

I move to his belt next, fumbling slightly with the buckle in my haste. Dom's breath hitches as I lower his zipper, and I glance up to find his eyes hooded with unbridled lust. He's allowing me this rare moment of control, and I'm drunk on the power–on watching him tense with the anticipation of it all. I push his pants down his legs slowly, lifting each foot and peeling off each sock until he's standing before me in just his boxers.

Fuck me, he's beautiful.

All hard lines and taut muscle, a smattering of dark hair trailing enticingly from his navel down to below his waistband. My eyes fixate on the obvious bulge in his underwear, and I lick my lips unconsciously. Suddenly, I'm at a loss on how to proceed. I want to touch him, to taste him, but I'm ready for him to take back the reins. So, I stupidly hesitate.

As if reading my mind, Dom's voice, low and rough, breaks the tentative silence. "Take off your clothes," he orders me. "Then get on your knees."

Pure, wanton desire licks down my spine at his commands. Any lingering reluctance evaporates completely as I hurry to comply, stripping myself so fast I almost topple over before sinking to my knees at his feet. I look up expectantly, meeting his heated gaze and silently begging him to keep going.

"Take them off," he grits out, as if holding himself back from going completely fucking feral.

I peel his boxers down his legs, and my mouth immediately starts to water at the sight of his impressive cock springing free. I lean forward eagerly, wrapping my lips around the glistening head before waiting for another instruction. His groan of pleasure tells me I've done the right thing, sending another wicked thrill through me as I take him deeper.

I'm hoping my enthusiasm makes up for any lack of finesse as I hungrily suck him down, tracing my tongue up the pulsing vein on the underside of his dick before swirling it around the tip. His taste is addictive. I lap up every drop of salty precum that seeps onto my tongue, relishing the power of having him so aroused.

Dom's fingers tangle in my hair, gripping my scalp like he's desperate to fuck my face with reckless abandon. But still, he gives me this moment to show him just how badly I want this. I push myself to do better, eyes watering as I take him as deep as I can.

"Fuck yes, Shiloh," Dom hisses above me. "You're so fucking good at that. *Shit.*" His fists clench suddenly, pulling me back until he slips from my lips with an audible *pop.* I look up confused, lips wet and chest heaving, to find his eyes blazing with hunger.

"I need to be inside you. *Now,*" he growls.

I scramble up onto the bed as fast as my shaking legs will carry me. "How do you want me?" I breathe.

He follows me wordlessly down onto the mattress, his strong hands grabbing one of my legs and swinging it over himself until I'm straddling his hips. I lean down, immediately claiming his lips with my own. His tongue sweeps forcefully into my mouth as his hand finds its way between my thighs.

I moan against his lips as he swipes his fingers through my dripping center, my hips grinding impatiently against his hand. Dom chuckles before plunging two fingers inside me, the sound vibrating through my chest where I'm pressed against his.

"What's the rush?" he murmurs against my lips. "I've got you, baby."

As much as I trust him to give me exactly what I need, I can't wait any longer. I reach down and wrap my fingers around his wrist, pulling his hand up to my mouth so I can suck off my own wetness. He hums his approval as he watches me, like I'm some kind of fascinating spectacle he can't look away from.

Dropping my hand back between my legs, I guide the head of his solid cock to my slick entrance and sink down slowly, savoring the delicious stretch as he fills me completely. His brow furrows as he lets a deep groan slip.

Dom's hands grip my hips tightly, but he still seems content to let me set the pace, like he's intrigued to see what I'll do when he's not pinning me down. Slowly, I begin to move, relishing the friction as I grind my clit against his pelvis.

My hands roam Dom's chest and abs, marveling at the unfamiliar sight of him reclined beneath me. His eyes never leave my face, watching me with a rapt intensity that has me feeling like a goddess.

As my confidence grows, I pick up the pace, my breasts bouncing as I ride him. Dom bucks up to meet me, matching my rhythm thrust for thrust. The tiny room fills with the sound of our labored breathing and the slapping of skin against skin.

I lean down to kiss him again, hungry for that total connection we never seized before. The new position has Dom hitting that spot inside me that has me almost passing out. "Oh *fuck*, Dom," I cry out, my nails digging into his shoulders.

"That's it, baby. Let me hear you," he pants, his own fingers sinking a punishing grip into my ass cheeks.

Our movements become frantic, both of us racing towards release. Molten heat coils low in my stomach, winding tighter with each thrust. When I finally tumble over the edge, it's with a moan of pure ecstasy. My thighs tremble violently as wave after wave ripples through me. Through the fog of an earth-shattering orgasm, I barely notice Dom's hips falter beneath me.

"Holy. Fucking. Shit. *Shy*," he groans, finally yanking my hips down until I'm fully impaled on his pulsing dick.

I collapse onto his chest, panting heavily as the after-shocks subside and my body goes entirely limp. Dom wraps his arms around me, holding me close as we both come down from our high. My eyes almost well up as he strokes my back tenderly, fingers tracing idle patterns on my skin. With his other hand, he gently sweeps my hair away from my face, planting a tender kiss on my temple.

We lie in comfortable silence for several minutes. I bask in the warmth of his embrace, stunned by how natural it feels to be held by him. This tenderness, this affection–it's so far beyond the purely physical hunger I'd thought it was when he first dared to kiss me.

The moment is eventually shattered by a loud rumble from my stomach. Dom's chest shakes with laughter beneath me.

"Hungry?"

I nod sheepishly against his sweat-slicked skin. "Starving, actually. I was too nervous about our little shopping trip to eat much of a lunch."

"We should find some dinner then," Dom says, starting to sit up with me still plastered to his torso. I hum contentedly, though I'm not quite ready to peel myself off him.

"Stay with me tonight?" I ask softly, hating how vulner-able I sound but needing him to know I don't want this to end.

He doesn't respond immediately. Soon enough, the silence is so agonizing I have to lift my head to read his expression. He gazes down at me, a soft smile tugging at the corners of his mouth.

"Of course," he finally replies, and just like that, the knot of anxiety in my stomach unravels to a silken ribbon. One I want to tie around him until we're tethered to each other forever.

Fucking hell, Shiloh. You need to chill.

22

DOMINIC

THE GRAY AFTERNOON light dances across Shiloh's face as she meticulously rearranges a group of jack-o'-lanterns for the tenth time in the entrance foyer of Fairchild Manor. Her brow is furrowed so deeply in concentration, I'm concerned she'll be left with a permanent crevice between her eyes.

I can't help but smirk at her intense focus on such a trivial task–it's endearing, really, how much she cares about every tiny detail of this overly-theatrical event.

"You know, if you stare at those pumpkins any harder, they might just spontaneously combust," I tease, placing another cluster of black candles on an ornate side table near the front door.

Shiloh tuts, turning to scowl at me over her shoulder. "Unlike *some* people, I actually give a damn about making this place look perfect."

I let a sarcastic chuckle slip, moving closer to adjust one of the pumpkins she's just placed. As expected, she furiously twists it back to the way it was. "Oh, I care about perfection. I just naturally achieve it with far less fuss."

She swats my hands away from her precise display, huffing in mock indignation though a smirk lifts one side of her smart mouth. "Keep your paws off my impeccably placed decor, Dominic, or I won't talk to you for the rest of the evening."

"You say that as if I'm supposed to be deterred," I mutter, too low for anyone to hear, should they pass by. "I've yet to see you drool around a ball-gag, Shy girl."

As I watch a deep blush creep up Shiloh's neck, my mind drifts contentedly to the week that's passed since we went shopping for costumes. Waking up next to Shiloh in the morning is an experience I would sell my soul to relive a million times over. The warmth of her naked body pressed against mine, the soft sound of her breathing in those moments before she's fully conscious, the way she plants light kisses on any part of my skin she can reach before eventually rolling out of bed–it's all a colossal improvement on my previous habit of picking her lock just to be near her while she slept.

And a much better sight than jerking off beneath her bed frame like a fucking creep.

"Hello? Earth to Dom," Shiloh's voice shakes me out of my smug musing. "I asked if you could grab more candles from the storage room. Unless you'd rather stand there daydreaming for the rest of the afternoon?"

I roll my eyes with a snort. "Yes, of course, Your Highness. Do you need anything else while I'm at it? Perhaps I could polish your crown or fetch your scepter?"

"I believe you mean my cauldron and witch's broom!" Shiloh's laughter follows me as I head toward the storage room. While I'm rummaging in one of the many boxes we've tucked out of sight, a distinct creak rings out from the floor above my head. I pause, confused as to why anyone would be upstairs right now. But I hear no further movement.

"Fucking old houses," I mutter to myself. I think I'd knock the whole thing down if the bones of my own home groaned at me periodically throughout the day.

I grab an armful of candles and make my way back to the entrance hall, where Shiloh is now fiddling with a garland of autumn leaves.

"Your offering, my liege," I say with an exaggerated bow, holding the candles outstretched for her to take.

She quirks an eyebrow at me. "Careful, Dom. People might start to think you're actually enjoying all this."

"Hell, that would ruin my entire reputation," I grumble.

Melanie's nasal shout cuts through my enjoyment of Shiloh's melodic giggle, immediately souring the lighthearted moment. "Okay, everyone! Let's regroup in the ballroom and run through the final checklist." I'm certain she's done nothing more than *observe* and offer *'helpful critique'* since she got here only an hour ago.

We grudgingly follow her instruction, joining the rest of the committee in the now fully decorated ballroom. The space is truly transformed with cobwebs draped from the crystal chandelier, elaborate masks adorn the walls, and an array of taxidermy critters sit clustered in various corners and on tables. The dead beasts were my idea—one that I suggested would tie into Shiloh's witchcraft theme while also freaking Melanie the fuck out.

I wish I'd caught her face on camera when she'd first set eyes on one of the stuffed foxes.

As our truly inconsequential leader begins running

through her notes on a glittery clipboard, the double doors suddenly burst open with a dramatic flourish. Cornelius sweeps into the room, his flowing black cape billowing behind him as he strides to the center of our group.

"What a spectacle you have prepared, ladies and gentlemen! Bravo!" he coos. "Now, before our guests begin to arrive, gather round, for I have a tale to tell. A tale of horror, of bloodshed, of a phantom so vengeful it returns year after year to claim new victims!"

I resist the urge to roll my eyes. Shiloh warned me the eccentric caretaker had a penchant for theatrics, but I'd hoped not to be subjected to a private performance.

"In these very hallowed halls," he goes on, gesturing wildly, "the Fairchild family once employed a butcher. A man of great skill with his cleaver but possessed by a cruel and twisted mind. Legend has it, he would lure unsuspecting victims to his chopping block, promising the finest cuts of meat money could buy."

The old fool pauses for dramatic effect, his eyes scanning the faces of his mostly bemused audience. I glance at Shiloh out of the corner of my eye, expecting to see the same placating smile lifting her lips, but her expression surprises me. She's gone weirdly pale, her eyes darting nervously around the room.

She can't really be swallowing this bullshit, can she?

"But indeed, it wasn't animal flesh he was after, was it? Oh no," Cornelius builds up to his finale. "It was *human* meat the monster craved. And on one fateful All Hallow's Eve, he was caught in the act by none other than Nathaniel Fairchild himself. The townspeople of our dear Avalon, in their rage and disgust, took justice into their own hands. It is said they used the Butcher's own cleaver to end his reign of bloody terror!"

A collective shudder runs through the group, peppered with the occasional amused snort. I have to admit, Cornelius knows how to command a room, even if I find his over-zealous fanaticism incredibly grating.

"But of course, as is so often the case with truly malevolent souls, death was not the end for the Butcher." The caretaker drops his tone to a stage whisper. "Every Halloween, as the veil between worlds grows thinnest, he returns to the Fairchild Estate. They say you can hear the scrape of a whetstone across his cleaver, the heavy thud of his footsteps through the cellars. And if you're not on your guard, if you wander these halls alone... well, let's just say the infamous Butcher is always on the hunt for fresh meat to add to his larder."

Once Cornelius finally finishes his tale, a slow clap ripples around the room. I join in only for the sake of not being called out, shaking my head at the ridiculousness of it all. But as I turn to share a pointed look with Shiloh, I notice her eyes are fixed on the ceiling. Her pale face is pinched with thinly veiled anxiety.

"Shiloh...you okay?" I murmur, leaning in close enough that no one else will hear the concerned edge to my voice.

She jumps, as if she's forgotten I was standing right next to her. "Huh? Oh, yeah. I'm fine! Just, um... you know, last-minute jitters about the ball and stuff."

Her smile is wide and forced, not reaching her wide eyes. I raise an eyebrow, as unconvinced by her assurance as I was by Cornelius' ghost story. But before I can press further,

Melanie claps her hands to demand everyone's attention again.

"Alright, enough tall tales," she chirps. "We've got a Halloween Ball to throw, people! Everyone go and do your last checks on your stations and then you can all go and change. Let's make this a night to remember!"

As the group disperses, I can't quite let go of the feeling that something's off with Shiloh. Her eyes keep darting to the ceiling, and she seems distracted, jumpy even. I want to pull her aside and demand to know what's wrong, to find out if there's anyone I have to stab for bothering her. But I know she wouldn't want us to appear too close in public. Not after the disaster in town with our parents.

When her eyes flit to the ceiling for what must be the tenth time in as many minutes, I follow her gaze with my own. I see nothing but ornate moldings and crystal chandeliers. Whatever's spooking her, it's not visible to the naked eye.

"Okay seriously, you sure you're alright?" I ask. "You seem freaked out. Don't tell me the old crank got to you."

Shiloh's snaps her head towards me. "Of course not," she answers, her voice a touch too bright. "I'm just excited to finally see it all come together. You know it's my favorite night of the year."

"*Right.* Because nothing says 'excited' like repeatedly checking the ceiling for...what, exactly? Stray cobwebs?"

She laughs and swats at my arm, but the sound is brittle, and I don't miss the slight tremor in her fingers. "Don't be silly, Dom. I'm just making sure everything's perfect. You were literally teasing me about it ten minutes ago."

"Well, if Avalon's judgment is all you're worried about, I'd say we're in pretty good shape. You've thrown together an event I wouldn't mind being seen at."

The taunt earns me a genuine chuckle this time. "Speaking of getting into shape," she says, brushing my arm again in a gesture that seems casual but leaves me aching for so much more, "we should probably start getting ready. Could you grab our costumes from the car, please? I said I'd help Jemma bring some dishes out from the kitchen before I get changed."

"Sure. But try not to rearrange the entire manor while I'm gone, okay?"

She rolls her eyes, but I catch the hint of a smile as I turn to head back towards the front door. The weather is uncharacteristically mild for this time of year, but as I make my way down the gravel drive to where I parked my car, I feel the hairs on the back of my neck suddenly stand on end.

I stop, that uneasy feeling of being watched settling over me like an itchy blanket. Slowly, I turn back towards the manor, my eyes scanning the windows for any sign of an observer. But the facade is still, the windows dark and empty, save for the flickering glow of candles on the ground floor.

Shrugging off the eerie sensation, I continue to my car. Shiloh's strange mood clearly has me on edge–I'm honestly starting to wonder if I know who the fuck I am anymore. I came to this town as a notoriously unshakable character, lording over every aspect of my life with confidence and precision. And now, here I am, feeling nervous before a damn costume party because the woman I care about will be devastated if it doesn't go off without a hitch.

The woman I care about...

The title rings hollow. Shiloh is so much more to me than that. Shiloh is *everything*.

I retrieve our garment bags and masks from the trunk, reminding myself that this is the man I have to be to make her happy. Maybe one day it won't feel like the role requires a mask of its own.

As I stride back to the house, I find myself mentally bracing for the night ahead. It's going to be a long evening of playing our parts–the barely cordial stepsiblings, the dutiful committee members. Every fiber of my being wants to wrap my arm around Shiloh and claim her in front of the whole town at once.

But that's not in the cards for us, at least not yet. For tonight, I have to be content with watching her twirl around the room with her friends, wrapped in rippling silk. Easily done with the promise of dragging her back to bed with me once this whole spectacle is over.

23

SHILOH

THE BALLROOM IS a swirling kaleidoscope of color and sound, filled with the rustle of costumes and the hum of excited chatter. Dom and I stand on the fringe of the crowd, both of us satisfied observers of the spectacle before us.

My chest swells with pride and relief to see the success we had a hand in creating. Weeks of planning, mind-numbing committee meetings, and one very awkward phone call to my estranged stepbrother have all led to this magical moment.

And if I drink enough, I might be able to tune out Melanie's gloating.

I turn to Dom, allowing myself a moment to appreciate how devastatingly sexy he looks in his costume. The flickering candlelight casts shadows across his chiseled features, while the perfect fit of his tailcoat has me wanting to sink my teeth into those deliciously broad shoulders.

"You know," I say, a slight smirk tugging at the corner of my mouth, "if your hair was a bit longer, you'd be the spitting image of Johnny Depp in Sleepy Hollow."

Dom's lips quirk just a little, though his eyes never leave

the crowd as he determinedly maintains an air of bored indif-ference. "I'll take that as a compliment. Though I must point out, that film was set over a century after the Connecticut witch trials. Are you accusing me of missing your theme, Oh Great Avalon Lore Expert?"

"Can't you just let a girl tell you that you look hot without being such a smartass?" I roll my eyes, nudging him with my elbow. "Although...if you wanna talk about missing the theme, Melanie will have your balls if you don't put that mask on."

He huffs a frustrated sigh, the final piece of his costume still hanging off his finger. "The fuck has my life become?" he mutters before pulling the elastic over his head. The mask is a twisted, black web of spray-painted wicker that obscures the top half of his face and reduces his eyes to glinting obsid-ian. I wouldn't be surprised if anyone mistook him for some pagan deity, this imposing creature that would give any sane human a heart attack if they came across him in the middle of a cornfield.

"Fuck me, that thing is terrifying...why am I turned on right now?" I speak low enough that only he can hear me as I stare wide-eyed at the monster that towers over me.

A low chuckle rumbles in his chest as he leans in close, his breath hot against my cheek. "I'm glad you like it. And you, my little Shy Girl, look tempting enough that every man and woman in this room would likely sell their soul to the devil, just for the chance to touch you."

Heat blooms across my cheeks, and I glance around nervously, suddenly hyper-aware of how close we're standing. Thankfully, the mask of swirling black lace I've fastened over my own eyes should obscure the worst of it. Otherwise, it might be obvious to passersby that my stepbrother is whispering salacious things to me right now.

My heart races with the desire to reach out and touch him, to claim him as mine in front of everyone. But I know I can't. The thought of being at the center of Avalon's scandal of the year makes my stomach churn.

"Behave yourself, Dominic," I murmur and take a sip of my drink, savoring the burn of alcohol as it slides down my throat. It's refreshing, though nothing seems to heat my veins quite as easily as the man standing next to me.

Our flirtatious bubble pops when I spot Ruby and Jemma pushing through the crowd toward us, their faces flushed with excitement and no doubt several drinks of their own.

"Shiloh!" Ruby calls out, grabbing onto my arm. "Come on, girly, you have to dance with us! The DJ is killing it tonight."

I hesitate for a moment, caught between the desire to stay with Dom and the pull of my best friends. Turning to him again, I ask, "Want to join us?"

The girls exchange confused looks, clearly surprised by my warmth toward the guy I ranted so furiously about only a couple of weeks ago.

Dom's face remains impassive as he shakes his head. "Dancing isn't really my thing. You go ahead."

Disappointment twists in my chest, but I paste on an understanding smile. It was a long shot anyway. I follow my friends to the dance floor, casting one last, longing glance over my shoulder at Dom's brooding figure.

The music pulses through me as I lose myself in the rhythm of the bass. Ruby and Jemma flank me either side, our bodies moving in sync as we twirl and laugh together like we have on so many wild nights at The Cauldron. For a little while, I forget about the pressure of organizing this event, the constant confusion of strange happenings that have plagued me in recent weeks, and the ever-present weight of my growing feelings for a man I'm not sure I can depend on.

When the beat transitions into a slower melody, I turn, breathless from all the dancing, and blanch a little as I'm met with Greyson's intense gaze.

"May I have this dance?" he asks, a hopeful smile playing on his lips as a hand extends toward me.

I hesitate, reading the not-so-innocent look in his eyes, but before I can politely decline, a hard body presses itself against my spine. Dom's voice cuts through the music, cold and sharp. "Ask someone else. Shiloh's not interested in you."

Greyson's face flushes a deep crimson as he sputters, "I-I wasn't...I didn't mean..."

With a dismissive wave of his hand, Dom talks over him. "Save it. Everyone can see you've had a pathetic crush on her for a while. It's time to let it go before you really embarrass yourself."

My eyes widen in shock at his blunt assault. "Dom! Can you shut the fuck up for a second?" I interject, thoroughly mortified. "I'm so sorry, Grey, you didn't deserve that. Can we talk about thi–"

Before I can even finish my sentence, Greyson mumbles something about getting another drink and hurries away. I whirl on Dom, anger bubbling up inside me. "That was a dick move. Greyson and I have been friends for years, I was going to let him down easy."

Instead of bothering to respond, Dom pulls me close as the slow song continues. His arm snakes around my waist, holding me firmly against him as he leans down and whispers, "I don't ever want to see another man's hands on you."

A molten heat licks down my spine at his words, and I struggle to maintain my disapproving expression. Part of me wants to push him away, to scold him for his caveman behavior. But another, more primal part of me, is thrilled at his possessive attitude. His confession feels almost...*permanent.*

We sway together, the tension between us palpable. I'm acutely aware of every point where our bodies touch–of the warmth of his hand on my exposed lower back and the intoxicating scent of his cologne. The rest of the crowd fades away until it's just us, moving gently to the music.

"What will happen now?" I whisper against his shoulder, too nervous to let him see the vulnerability in my eyes. "This whole Ball business is over and done with...Will you go back to New York soon?"

I feel his body stiffen ever so slightly, the hand on my spine clenching into a tight fist before relaxing again only a second later. "I haven't figured out the details yet," he mutters into my hair. "My father has been threatening to send a hunting party if I don't return to the company soon. But who knows...Maybe I'll sell my shares and leave. Or maybe I'll take over and you can come and join me, you wouldn't have to work anymore if you didn't want to."

My jaw almost hits the floor at his suggestion, my lips gaping open with an audible *pop!* I've barely sorted out my own feelings about everything that's happened between us, and he's been thinking about us living together in the future?

"Dom... I, um, I don't know what to–"

"There you are!" We spring apart as Melanie's shrill greeting almost bursts my ear drum. "I've been looking everywhere for you, Dominic! We need your help judging the costume contest. I'm sure I must have mentioned it to you!"

Dom stares at her blankly, his expression betraying nothing of the fierce annoyance I know he must be feeling. "I'm not interested."

But Melanie, the ever-persistent first daughter of our humble town, doesn't back down without a fight. "Oh, come now. You're our generous sponsor! Judging the contest is part of your role."

I bite back a giggle at Dom's obvious displeasure. "She's right, Dom," I say, unable to resist the urge to tease him a little. "You should go help." I don't feel like adding that I'm not quite ready to iron out the details of whatever future he's supposedly envisioning for the two of us.

The glare he shoots me could melt reinforced steel, but I simply smile innocently in return. With visible reluctance and a grumbled goodbye, he follows Melanie, leaving me alone in the middle of the dance floor.

As I watch him disappear into the crowd, I can't help but feel my amusement overshadowed by something deeper, more visceral. Even as I threw him to the wolves–or rather, to a simpering Melanie–a part of me already craves his return.

Turns out I'm royally fucking fucked, I guess. Surely, I'm not about to pack up and skip town for this guy... I wouldn't do that... Would I?

The swirling possibilities bounce off the inside of my skull until a dull ache has formed at my temples. I decide I desperately need some air, though that's as far ahead as I can think right now. Slipping away from the raucous crowd, I make my way through the entrance hall and out into the frigid night.

The grounds of Fairchild Manor are eerily quiet compared to the bustling party inside. Moonlight casts long shadows across the overgrown lawn, and a light mist is rolling in from the woods beyond. It's not a cornfield, but still a very ideal setting for a horror movie. It makes me smile–but it quickly fades.

As if on cue, I spot a figure in the distance, creeping out from the enormous shadow cast by the manor itself. They're shrouded in a hooded cloak and wielding something that glints in the bluish glow of the moon. For a split second, my heart races with genuine fear, my muscles seizing with the memory of the last couple of times I've seen a figure suddenly appear on this estate. But then I remember that I'm at a fucking costume party, and hundreds of people here are cloaked and masked. I chuckle to myself with a shake of my head.

Whoever it is gets steadily closer, before pausing on the grass maybe twenty feet from me and raising that shiny object in the air. It's a meat cleaver. Or, at least, it's probably a *fake* meat cleaver, not unlike the one that Dom chased me through the house with that day we ended up in the library.

I hope this mystery person doesn't expect a similar happy ending.

I snort at the thought and raise my hand to wave, ready to congratulate the guest on their costume. But they don't wave back. They just stand there, as if they're watching me from beneath that hood. The silent face off lasts long enough that I start to get a little uncomfortable...

Why the fuck are they out here in the grounds instead of enjoying the party inside? And why are they just standing there instead of saying hi? Everyone in this town knows each other...

"Alright then," I mutter to myself, turning to make my way back inside and leave whoever it is to their creepy vigil.

But the moment I take the first step, the mystery figure launches into a sprint. Heading straight for me.

"Nope!" I yelp, long since sick of being chased around this damn place. I shoot back toward the house, my heels sinking into the grass with every laborious step.

I barely make it a few feet before they tackle me, a small shriek bursting from my lips as I fall to the damp ground.

"What the fuck?" I shout, wriggling furiously until I can flip onto my back and shove the asshole off. In the scuffle, their hood falls back, revealing a grotesque rubber mask of a snarling man dripping in blood.

It takes me half a second to notice the erratic tufts of gray hair sticking out from all over the guy's head. "Cornelius?! Is that *you*?"

"Got you good, didn't I?" his gleeful chirp seeps from behind the mask. "Beware of the Butcher! Ha ha ha! Happy Halloween!"

He scampers away too fast for me to plant my foot between his legs, leaving me raging in the damp grass. "If there is mud on my dress, I will cut a bitch," I grumble to myself as I clamber to my feet.

The adrenaline soon drains from me, leaving me exhausted and my feet aching from trying to run in stilettos. With a low groan, I begin a slow dawdle back towards the front of the house, remembering that I left a pair of flat ballet pumps in Dom's car for this exact reason.

Thank fuck he asked me to put his key in my purse.

I find Dom's car easily in the nearest corner of the adjoining field and pop the trunk. With a sigh, I start rummaging through its contents. In my search, I pull out a backpack, unsure as to where Dom might have shoved my shoes while he was packing up our costumes this morning.

But when I pull down the zipper, I don't find a pair of shoes inside. Instead, I come across a leather notebook. *My* notebook...one of my old journals. Except it's not just one. It's *all* of them. Every single one.

The faded diaries I poured my heart into for years are sitting in Dom's trunk. My blood runs cold. *How the fuck did he get these? And why does he have them?*

Excruciating memories suddenly flash through my mind like vicious forks of lighting, and my stomach starts to churn. I'm flooded with all the times I'd written about him, about *us*–the fantasies, the fears, the deepest parts of myself I never intended anyone else to see.

And he's read all of it.

I'm still standing paralyzed, struck dumb with shock when I hear footsteps crunching across the gravel beyond the fence.

"There you are," Dom's voice calls out. "I've been looking everywhere for you."

The casual familiarity in his voice only fuels the rage building inside me. I hold up the journal in my hand, almost shaking with the urge to launch it at his head. "What the fuck is this, Dominic?"

His expression changes instantly, guilt flashing across his features before he schools them into careful neutrality. It's all the confirmation I need.

"How could you?" I demand, my voice cracking on the last word. "Did you steal these from my house?"

Dom reaches for me, but I instantly back away, stumbling on the uneven ground. "Shiloh, listen–"

"Don't touch me!" I explode. "Why did you really come to town, Dom? Why did you stay? Was this all just some sick game to you? To fuck with me?" A steady stream of tears worms its way down my cheeks. He's betrayed every last drop of trust he's managed to leech from me since the day he sauntered into that coffee house.

And I can't fucking *stand him* for it.

24

DOMINIC

"IT MAY HAVE STARTED out that way," I answer calmly, resigned to this all coming out right here and now. "I came to town after you called because I wanted to see you suffer up close... You were right before, I was bored."

Shiloh's eyes widen, her tears not letting up for a second as she processes my words. I watch a parade of emotions play across her features one after the other–disbelief, pain, and finally, the resurgence of that red-hot anger she was shaking with when I found her out here.

The only small mercy I have right now is that she seems too in shock to yell anymore.

"I followed you that night after we met at the coffee house," I press on, the raw confession feeling like I'm flaying off my own skin. "I heard everything you said about me at The Cauldron...I was...I don't know. I guess I was furious, but I couldn't bring myself to leave. That night was the first time I broke into your house."

"The first time..." Shiloh repeats my admission in a broken whisper, and I can almost see the cogs turning in her skull. She no doubt is putting together I was the one moving her things around the entire time, not some lovesick student. She rakes her hands through her hair, mussing the curls she spent forever styling, her sobs coming thick and fast. "I should have known I c-couldn't trust you. I should've known th-that this *new*, *kind* version of you was all a lie. What is wrong with you? You sick fuck!" Every word comes out a little more shrill until she's screaming at me again, clutching her diary to her chest like a shield.

"I know it was wrong, okay? I know that!" Despite my best efforts, I can't help but raise my own voice, too anxious for her to just calm down and hear me out. "I don't know what came over me, I was just...I was *obsessed*, Shy! I didn't want to let you out of my sight. Seeing you again after so many years I...I had this *craving*."

I can only pray she sees the truth of it all in my face. I tear the ridiculous mask off and toss it to the ground, letting her see the honesty I'm trying so desperately to convey in my eyes. "It started out as just wanting to fuck with you, but then I found your diaries from when we were kids and...*Fuck,* I just wanted to know... I wanted to know if you felt the same way about me that I've always felt about you. *Always.*"

"You want to know how I feel, Dom?" Shiloh spits. "I feel *sick.* I feel like a complete fucking idiot for letting you get anywhere near me. I let you *touch me.* Fuck off back to New York and leave me the hell alone." She tries to storm past me then, her legs wobbling as she maneuvers the damp ground in those thin heels. The finality in her tone is a dagger to my chest, leaving me torn open and bleeding.

I can't let this be the end. I won't.

"No," I bite out, wrapping my fingers around her bicep and pulling her back to me. "I'm not letting you go, not now."

Shiloh scoffs, her laugh bitter and cutting as she shoves against my chest with all her strength. "Letting me go? You don't *own* me, asshole. I'm not yours to keep and I sure as fuck never will be."

I don't release my grip on her arm, ignoring how she struggles against me. "Just stop for a minute. I know I fucked up, but I want you in my future, Shy. *Please.*"

She flinches at the nickname. "Don't call me that," she hisses. "You've lost that right."

When she gives my chest another fierce push, I finally let go, unable to let myself keep her trapped–even if it might break me to see her walk away. "Please, just listen–"

Shiloh slaps me right across the cheek, her palm connecting with a sharp sting. "Listen to what? More lies? More *bullshit*?"

The agony in her eyes is almost the death of me. I want to gather her in my arms, to promise her that I'll never hurt her again–but I know that's not what she needs right now. She needs the truth, all of it, no matter how humiliating.

"I'm not lying to you, not anymore," I say, forcing my voice to stay even. "Every fucked-up thing I did was because I wanted to be close to you. I know that's no excuse, but I was desperate to *know* you, to *understand* you. I convinced myself that reading your diaries was the only way to do that."

"You're right, that's not an excuse," Shiloh snaps, though she's not running away from me anymore. She breathes a ragged inhale, fists clenching and unclenching around the journal. After a few moments, her shoulders sag slightly, some of the fight draining out of her right in front of me. "I thought...I thought I was falling in love with you." She's whispering now, her voice cracking around another sob.

"Shiloh..." I grab her hand. Hope flares in my chest, but I squash it down. Hope is a fool's game.

She shakes her head, sniffling profusely. "I can't imagine ever trusting you again."

"You can–"

"No, *enough*. If you don't let me go right now, I will fucking scream."

"Where are you going?" I call out as she storms past me, acidic panic rising in my throat.

Shiloh spins back to face me, her eyes blazing with a fury that eclipses any I've ever seen from her–any I thought her capable of. "I'm going *away* from you. I can't stand to look at your face anymore."

I can only watch her go, every fiber of my being screaming to follow her, to make this right. But I know that chasing her now will likely end with me being driven out of town by a crowd armed with torches and pitchforks. I've made a mess of everything, and for the first time in my life...

I care enough to want to fix it.

But I have no fucking clue how.

I lean against my car, the cold metal biting at my skin through my clothes. Clawing my hands through my hair again, I tug at the roots as if the pain might clear my head. "Fuck, fuck, *fuck*," I mutter, each word punctuated by a fresh wave of self-loathing.

I'd stashed those journals in my trunk days ago, so sure I'd be able to return them before she ever knew they were missing. I thought I'd just slip them back into that dusty box under her stairs, and she'd be none the wiser. But somewhere along the way I'd forgotten, my whole world tilted on its axis with every second Shiloh opened up to me a little more.

"You fucking idiot," I growl, chiding myself. My fist connects with the hood of my car before I even realize I'm moving. The dull thud of impact is followed by a sharp sting in my knuckles, but the pain is welcome. It's something to focus on, because I can't handle the crushing weight of watching her leave.

I have *to fix this.*

The version of my future where I drive back to New York and never see Shiloh again is one I'll die before I accept.

25

SHILOH

I STALK off into the tree line past the manor, desperate for just five minutes to catch my breath. The freezing night air whips at my bare skin, but I barely notice it through the storm of emotions raging inside me. Dom's confession replays in my mind over and over, a broken record of guilt and insanity that leaves me wanting to throw up.

Pacing back and forth between two towering oaks, I wrap my arms around my body as if I can physically stop myself from completely falling apart. I don't know what the hell I'm supposed to do with all of this. I feel like I'm on one of those true crime documentaries–the naïve little stepsister who ends up buried beneath the floorboards.

But no matter how furious I feel–how betrayed–I can't reconcile Dom's face with that of the psychopath who would do any of this. The vulnerability in his eyes as he laid his soul bare to me...It was so raw, so real.

I've seen that look before... It was there when we were wrapped up in each other's bodies, and when he held me with more tenderness than anyone else ever has. Regardless of how much I hated him when he sauntered into town, I can't deny he's changed.

Or has he just manipulated me so well I have fucking Stockholm Syndrome?

A twig snaps behind me, and I stop my pacing, still hugging myself tight as I stare into the blackness of the woods in front of me. The sound of crunching leaves follows, steady footsteps approaching. I should have known that Dom wouldn't leave me to stew too long, in case I talk myself out of ever forgiving him.

I don't turn around. I can't face him just yet. Instead, I take a deep breath and start talking, the words tumbling out before I can lock them away forever.

"I don't know how to deal with everything you told me yet, Dom." My voice comes out rasping, my throat raw from all the sobbing, but I swallow hard and push on. "Honestly, I'm just so fucking mortified you read all those pathetic journal entries. All that teenage angst and whining and..and how I pined for you."

The footsteps come to a stop just behind me. I can feel the warmth radiating from his body, hear his soft exhale of breath. Then, he strokes his knuckles down my bare arms, sending a shiver down my spine that has nothing to do with the cold.

My eyes flutter closed, and I can't help the sigh that escapes my lips. "This is so fucked up," I whisper, leaning into him slightly. "But I can't lie about how I feel when you touch me. I've craved you for so long...longer than I want to admit, even to myself."

Warm lips press into my shoulder, feather-light and achingly tender. I take another deep breath, barely believing

I'm about to do this. But I don't think I have a choice. I can't find it in me to push him away again. I turn to face him, my heart pounding so hard I swear he must be able to hear it battering against my ribcage.

But the face that greets me is not Dom's.

A skeletal mask leers down at me from beneath a black hood. I shriek, stumbling backward and shoving at the stranger with what little strength I have left. But they're faster, stronger. Before I can blink, they tackle me to the ground, leaves and twigs stabbing into the skin of my exposed back.

A blood-curdling scream tears from my throat and I thrash wildly as the monster paws at me. They claw at the bodice of my gown, trying to force it down and expose my breasts. Panic floods my system like shards of ice ripping me apart from the inside. I buck harder, desperate to throw them off.

"Help!" I cry, my broken voice seeming to just fade into the empty trees. "Somebody help me!"

The masked assailant gives up on my boned corset, failing to tear it from my flesh. But there is no relief, no protection as their hand plunges lower, scrabbling at my skirts and trying to force their way between my legs.

Every muscle in my body seizes to cold stone. It's all I can do to keep breathing, knowing exactly what's about to happen. I squeeze my eyes shut, bracing for the worst.

Suddenly, the weight on top of me vanishes in one fell swoop. My eyes fly open just in time to see a blur of motion as my attacker is ripped away. I scramble backward, the soles of my feet torn and bleeding while my kicked-off shoes lie several feet away.

Shuddering sobs wrack my entire body as the scene before me comes into focus.

Dom has my attacker pinned to the ground, raining blow after savage blow on their face. The skeleton mask shatters under his fists, revealing glimpses of bloody flesh beneath. As the pieces fall away, my stomach drops, recognition dawning like sharpened claws raked across my flesh.

"Dom, stop!" I yell, hoarse and breathless. But he doesn't seem to hear me. He just keeps punching, a low growl emanating from deep in his chest.

Though it's now a mess of blood and already-swelling bruises, there's no mistaking the face of Jake Pearson, the mouthy jock from the sophomore class.

"Stop it! He's a student," I choke out. "You're going to kill him!"

But Dom is lost in a haze of rage, his fists continuing their relentless assault. Jake's whimpers grow weaker, and real fear grips me. This isn't justice–it's vengeance. And if someone doesn't stop it soon, Dom could cross a line he can never come back from.

Just as I'm about to throw myself between them, a small crowd bursts through the trees. Greyson is at the front, his eyes wide as he searches through the gloom for the source of all the chaos. Without hesitation, he lunges forward and grabs Dom, yanking him off Jake's limp form.

Dom snarls again, struggling against Greyson's hold. But then his eyes lock onto mine, and the fight drains out of him instantly. He shoves away from Greyson and rushes to my side, falling to his knees beside me.

"Are you okay?" he demands, his hands hovering over me,

searching for injuries and unsure where to land. "Did he hurt you? Shiloh, talk to me!"

I can't form words. The adrenaline is wearing off, leaving me shaky, nauseated, and freezing. Instead, I throw myself into Dom's arms, clinging to him as I shudder, fresh tears soaking into his jacket. He holds me tightly, murmuring soothing words into my hair.

From the corner of my blurred vision, I see a pair of men drag Jake's semi-conscious form away. The gathered crowd is buzzing with shocked whispers and half-formed questions. But all I can focus on is the solid warmth of Dom's chest against my cheek, the steady thrum of his heartbeat lulling me into an exhausted kind of numbness.

After what feels like hours but is probably only minutes, Dom gently helps me up from the dirt. My legs are unsteady, and I hiss when I put weight on my abused feet. Without a word he sweeps me up into his arms, glaring daggers at anyone who dares step too close.

"What the hell happened?" Greyson demands, his wide eyes darting between my trembling form and Dom's murderous expression.

I take a shaky breath, trying to form a coherent string of words despite the cloying fog of shock invading my senses. "It was J-Jake. Jake Pearson," I croak. "I think he's the one who has been terrorizing people around the manor in that cloak. He's shown up twice in the past couple of weeks while I've been here alone, and tonight he tried to... to..."

Dom's arms tighten around me as I fail to get the words out. His jaw is clenched as he adds, "He probably sent you those flowers too. It wasn't me."

My head snaps up to look at him, the sickening revelation

almost too much to bear. But before I can even fully absorb the implications, Ruby, Jemma, and Luke push their way to the front of the crowd, their faces contorted with worry.

"Oh my God, Shiloh!" Ruby cries, reaching for my hand. "Are you alright?"

I nod weakly, even though I'm anything but alright. "I'll be fine," I insist, curling tighter into Dom's chest. "Can you...can you just take me home, please?"

He doesn't hesitate, already striding away from the prying eyes and whispered speculations. "Yeah, let's get you out of here."

"You'll probably both be wanted for statements," Greyson pipes up.

"Shut the fuck up before I pulverize your face too," Dom snarls, pushing past him. The rest of the gathered onlookers part, cringing back as if Dom were carrying some infectious disease instead of a trembling assault victim.

The drive home passes too slowly, my blood feeling like thick tar as it pulses weakly through my body. Dom keeps one hand on my knee, a steady, grounding presence as I stare out the window, unseeing. When we finally pull up to my house, I fumble with the seatbelt, my fingers clumsy and uncooperative.

Dom comes around to my side of the car, wordlessly lifting me again before he makes his way to the front door. Inside, I stand in the middle of my living room, suddenly unsure what to do with myself. I'm still in my gown, the fabric now dirty and torn in places. My eyes well up again as I try to untangle the shredded ties.

"Here, let me help you with that," Dom murmurs softly, moving behind me to start unlacing the ribbons that now feel like a cage. His touch is achingly gentle, as if he's worried I might shatter into a million pieces right here on the rug. "You should probably take a shower, get cleaned up. It might help you feel better."

I nod numbly, but as he finishes with the laces and steps away, panic seizes me all over again. I spin around, grabbing his wrist. "Will you..." I swallow hard, hating how small and scared my voice sounds. "Will you stay? Will you still be here when I get out?"

Dom's hard shoulders drop just a fraction, his relief palpable as he reaches up to cup my cheeks. "Of course," he says without hesitation. "I'll stay as long as you want me here, Shy."

I can't think of what to say next, so I just collapse forward and thread my arms around his waist, holding on for dear life. Dom cradles my head against his chest, his heart beating an erratic rhythm against my ear. For a long moment, we just stand in silence, his other hand rubbing soothing circles over my grazed back.

Eventually, Dom speaks, his lips brushing against my forehead. "I love you, Shiloh. I'll do anything to earn back your trust. *Anything.*"

The whirlwind of emotions that sweeps through me would have me crumbling to my knees were it not for his strong arms holding me up. There's a mixture of hope, doubt, longing, and fear, but beneath it all, there's a certainty I can't ignore. "I love you too," I admit. "Lord knows I'm questioning my own sanity, but I do. I love you... And I want you to stay."

Dom presses a tender kiss into my hair but doesn't speak again. It takes me a minute or two to realize that he never heard any of those words I spoke into the trees when I thought he was behind me.

"I want to trust you again," I mumble into his shirt. "But you can't lie to me again, Dom. And you can't leave me alone like you did the first time. I can't go through that again. You were gone for eleven years too fucking long."

""I'm not going anywhere," he vows, his deep voice rumbling through me and somehow thawing my aching muscles. "No matter where we end up, I'll be by your side."

I squeeze him tighter, feeling truly safe for the first time all night. Maybe for the first time in a long time. Before the exhaustion sets in deep enough that I won't make it to the shower, I find myself exhaling a shuddering sigh. "Maybe it's just me...but Avalon might not be the right place for either of us anymore."

Dom's answering huff is equal parts bitter and grudgingly amused. "Maybe not. We can figure out a fresh start anywhere you want to go."

We stay like that a little longer, holding each other close as the weight of the last month's events and our naked confessions settles around us. Hardly anything feels resolved, and yet somehow, I can't find it in me to worry about the rest of it.

Dom wants to stay with me. And maybe despite myself, I trust that he means it. Right now, there's nothing else I need. There's nothing else I've ever needed more than someone who just fucking stays. I drag him up the stairs with me, not wanting even a second apart.

It might seem like everything has changed in that regard...

But nothing really has.

Nothing ever does.

EPILOGUE

SHILOH'S HAND is warm in mine as we weave through the crowded fairground, the scent of candy floss and roasted nuts thick in the air.

"Baby, look!" Shiloh tugs on my arm, pointing to an elaborate display of animatronic witches cackling over a steaming cauldron. "So fucking cool!"

I nod absentmindedly, more captivated by the way her eyes dance with childlike wonder than the admittedly impressive Halloween setup. "It's not bad," I concede, allowing a small smile to tug at my lips.

We've been at this fair for hours now, and Shiloh's enthusiasm hasn't waned for a second. It's infectious, really. I find myself actually enjoying the tacky decorations and overpriced games, if only because they bring her such joy.

As we pass a ring toss booth, the bloody scarecrow behind the counter calls out to us in that bizarre sort of garbled British accent I still can't get used to. "Step right up, sir! Win a prize for the lovely lady?"

I'm about to decline when Shiloh squeezes my hand. "Oh, come on, Dom. Have a go!"

With a dramatic sigh that makes her giggle, I hand over a five pound note and accept the plastic rings. "You know these games are rigged, right?"

Shiloh just shrugs, her grin widening. "Then I guess you'll have to use those legendary negotiation skills of yours, won't you?"

I can't help but chuckle at that. It still blows my mind how different my life is now compared to a year ago. No more board-room battles or high-stakes deals. Just this–traveling the world with the woman I love, chasing whatever whim strikes our fancy.

To my surprise, I manage to land two of the five rings on the bottlenecks. It's probably not enough to win the oversized stuffed animal Shiloh's eyeing, but the scarecrow seems impressed.

"Not bad, mister! How about we make it double or noth-ing? Land one more and you can have any prize on the top shelf."

I glance at my girl, who's practically bouncing with excite-ment. "What do you think, baby? Should I risk it?"

She nods emphatically, and I turn back to the scarecrow with a confident smirk. "You're on."

The ring sails through the air, wobbling slightly before settling around the neck of a bottle with a satisfying clink. Shiloh lets out a whoop of joy, throwing her arms around me. "Oh shit, you did it! You actually did it!"

Holding her tight, I breathe in the berry scent of her hair. "Of course I did. I always get what I want, don't I?"

She pulls back, a mischievous glint in her eye. "Is that so?

Then I want that one." She points to an enormous plush bat with cartoonishly large eyes.

The scarecrow hands it over, and Shiloh immediately buries her face in its soft fur. "I'm going to name him Vlad."

I roll my eyes again but can't keep the fondness out of my voice. "Of course you are."

"Oh! Cotton candy!" She's already dragging me towards a nearby vendor, fishing in her purse for her wallet. I swear, she turns into a toddler at these things.

I beat her to it, handing over a crisp note before she can protest. "My treat."

The vendor–a pale-skinned Dracula–passes over an enormous cloud of pink spun sugar, and Shiloh wastes no time tearing into it. I watch, bemused, as she devours the confection with gusto, leaving a sticky residue all over her lips and fingers.

"Want some?" she mumbles around a mouthful, holding out the rapidly diminishing treat.

I shake my head. "I'll leave the sugar high to you, thanks."

Shiloh shrugs, popping another piece into her mouth. "Your loss. This stuff is heaven."

"I'm more interested in how you manage to eat your body weight in sugar and still keep this tight ass," I tease, running my hand down her side before giving said ass a playful spank. She swats at me away with a muffled laugh, still chowing down on her tenth dessert of the evening.

We wander past more carnival games and food stalls, eventually finding ourselves in front of the ominous-looking structure with "*HAUNTED HOUSE*" spelled out in dripping, blood-red letters.

Shiloh's eyes light up. "Oh, we have to go in again!"

I raise an eyebrow at her. "Again? We've already been through twice."

"Third time's the charm," she insists, tugging on my arm. "Come on, it'll be fun."

"We already know every scare," I point out bluntly, even as I allow her to pull me towards the entrance. "Where's the thrill in that?"

Shiloh's grin turns devious. "Who says we have to be the ones getting scared? Imagine how funny it would be if *I* jumped out at *them* instead!"

I can already picture the chaos that would ensue–fake zombies and ghouls scrambling away from my pint-sized terror of a girlfriend. The mental image is almost enough to make me agree on the spot.

I chew on my cheek for a moment, already knowing I've lost this battle. "Fine. But when we get kicked out and banned for life, I'm blaming you."

Shiloh's victorious whoop draws curious glances from nearby fairgoers. She throws her arms around my neck, peppering my face with sticky, cotton candy-flavored kisses. "You're the best, you know that?"

"I do know that, actually," I reply dryly, but I can't keep the smile off my face. "Now come on, let's go terrorize some minimum wage workers."

Several hours and countless scares later, we're finally pulling up to the quaint cottage we've rented for our stay here in Cornwall, England. The narrow, tree-lined road is bathed in moonlight, casting eerie shadows that would be right at home in any of the horror movies Shiloh loves so much.

As I cut the engine, Shiloh is already unbuckling her seat-belt, practically vibrating with excitement. "That may have been the best Halloween date night *ever*," she gushes. "But we need to get some sleep before the best part of this whole trip tomorrow. Did you know the Museum of Witchcraft and Magic has over three thousand objects and books related to folk magic and witchcraft? There's even a recreation of a witch's cottage!"

I smirk at her enthusiasm, vaguely wondering how much I truly smiled before I sauntered back into this adorable woman's life. "Is that so?" I ask, playing along as we stroll up the charming garden path.

Shiloh nods emphatically, following me to the cottage door. "And they have all sorts of exhibits on the history of magical practice in Cornwall. Did you know this area was known for its *'pellers'*–people who used charms and rituals to heal the sick?"

"I did not," I admit, turning the key in the stiff, old-fashioned lock. "But I'm sure I'll know all about it by the time we leave."

Shiloh cackles, unrepentant. "You bet you will! I've got our whole itinerary planned out. We're going to learn so much!"

As the door swings open, revealing the cozy interior of our temporary home, an idea strikes me for how to manage her seemingly unlimited energy before we finally call it a night. I set the keys down on the table just inside the threshold and turn to Shiloh, placing my hands on her shoulders to stop her from darting inside.

I lean down, my lips brushing against her ear as I whisper, "Thirty seconds...*Run and hide.*"

Her eyes widen comically as I straighten up again. Without hesitation, she leaps past me, her giggles echoing through the cottage as she disappears from view.

I close my eyes, counting down slowly. "Thirty... twenty-nine... twenty-eight..." The familiar thrill of the hunt courses through my veins. "Three... two... one." My eyes snap open, a predatory grin spreading across my face. "Ready or not, here I come, Shy Girl."

I move through the cottage with deliberate slowness, listening for any telltale sounds. A loud creak rings out from above me and I chuckle to myself as I ascend the stairs, my footsteps purposefully heavy on the old wood.

"Oh, Shy Girl," I call out, my voice low and teasing. "Where could you be hiding?"

A muffled giggle from the bedroom gives her away. She would truly make a terrible criminal. I push the door open, quickly scanning the room. The edge of her shoe peeking out from under the bed is enough to make me sigh with disappointment at her pathetic attempt to evade capture.

In one swift motion, I drop to my knees and reach under the bed, my hands closing around her ankles. Shiloh shrieks with laughter as I drag her out, all the while scrabbling for purchase on the carpet.

"Caught you," I growl playfully, pinning her beneath me.

Shiloh squirms, still laughing breathlessly. "No fair," she protests. "You always find me too quickly."

I lean down, nuzzling at her neck. "Maybe you're just not very good at hiding, baby."

She huffs indignantly, but her retort is cut off as I capture her lips in a hungry kiss. The taste of candy and popcorn still lingers on her tongue, sickeningly sweet but somehow addictive when mixed with the taste of *her*.

When I pull back, Shiloh's cheeks are flushed, her blue eyes bright with desire. The sight of her like this–disheveled, panting, and all mine–sends a surge of primal yearning through me so strong, my brain short circuits.

The words tumble out before I can stop them. "Marry me."

Shiloh's glistening lips pop open in shock. "What? Did you just...?"

"Marry me," I repeat, more firmly this time. It's not really a question –she's always preferred my commands.

"Are you...are you serious?" she stammers. "You're not fucking with me?"

I shake my head, suddenly mad at myself for going about this all wrong. "I had it all planned out," I admit. "Romantic dinner tomorrow night, giant diamond hidden away in my underwear drawer... But I couldn't wait. I don't want to wait another second to make you mine in every way possible."

Tears well up in Shiloh's eyes, and for a heart-stopping moment, I worry I've miscalculated. But then she's nodding, a radiant smile splitting her face until I can practically count all her teeth.

"Yes," she breathes. "Yes, of course I'll marry you!"

Relief and joy flood through me in equal measure. I devour her lips again, pouring every ounce of love and passion I feel for this woman into the searing kiss.

Sick of kneeling on the floor, I stand abruptly, pulling my new fiancée up with me. She lets out a surprised squeak as I lift her off her feet and toss her onto the bed before crawling over her.

Shiloh hums her contentment, wrapping her arms around my neck and pulling me close. "I can't believe this is happening," she murmurs against my lips. "We're actually getting married. You and me."

I trail kisses along her jaw, reveling in the soft sounds she makes. "Believe it, Shy Girl. You're stuck with me forever."

Running her fingers through my hair, she tugs gently at my scalp to make me look at her. "How do you think Charlie and Viv will take the news?"

I consider it for a moment. Our parents' reactions to our relationship have been...*hesitant*, to say the least. But things have been improving, slowly but surely.

"Well," I eventually say, dipping down to kiss her temple, "they did invite us to Thanksgiving in Avalon. That's got to be a good sign, right?"

"I suppose so...Do you think they're really coming around to the idea of us being together? That it's not some gross crime?"

I pull back slightly, meeting her worried gaze again. "I think they're trying. They don't really have a choice. It's either get over it or never see us again. Not that they have ever cared that much about keeping us close..."

She snorts at that unfortunate truth, but I can see the hope in her eyes as she chews on her bottom lip. "Alright... Avalon Thanksgiving it is. And then what? What's next for the future Mr. and Mrs. Blackwood? More travel? Settling down somewhere?"

I haven't got an immediate answer for her. The truth is, I haven't thought much beyond making Shiloh my wife. The details seem inconsequential as long as we're together. After selling my shares in Blackwood Enterprises and nailing several perfectly timed investments, we're more or less set for life. Not many people can say that before they've even turned thirty.

"Whatever you want," I tell her honestly. "I don't care where we go or what we do, as long as I'm with you."

Shiloh's expression softens, tearing up again. "I love you," she whispers, the naked truth of it glistening in those crystalline eyes of hers.

"I love you too, baby. In my own twisted way, I always have. That will never change."

ALSO BY ANNIE WILD

No Control: A Dark Stalker Romance

Killing Emma: A Dark Captive Romance

The Huntress and Her Hound: A Dark Serial Killer Romance

The Wrong Drive: A Dark Holiday Romance

ABOUT THE AUTHOR

I love creating mostly slow burn, dark, suspenseful, and broody romances that question just how far into the gray we're willing to go for love.

When I'm not creating morally gray men and writing their redemptive arcs, you can find me going for hikes in the woods with my four dogs or immersing myself in a true crime podcast.

Printed in Dunstable, United Kingdom